"Is it almost time, Mommy?"

Olivia looked over at her son. His ruffled blond locks and paint-stained fingers tugged something inside her, and the worry started to knot in her stomach again.

"Not long now, honey. He'll be here soon."

She moved over to sit with her son and squeezed his hand.

"Will I like him?"

"Your dad? Of course! You'll love him, Charlie."

Her boy nodded and twisted his mouth into a smile. "Will he like me?"

Olivia laughed and gave him a soft play-punch on the arm. "Have you ever met anyone who didn't adore you?"

Charlie jumped up then, his eyes wide. "Did you hear that?"

Olivia's eyes fluttered shut for a heartbeat. Yes, she'd heard it, and if it wasn't for her son she might just have fled the scene. When they opened she was sitting at the table alone. The "Welcome Home Daddy" poster lay spread out in front of her, the splotches of paint and glitter a blur to her eyes.

This was it.

In less than thirty seconds, if the slam of a car door was anything to go by, her husband would be stepping back into her life. Would be seeing his son for the first time in two years.

Dear Reader

When I decided to write this book it was almost reluctantly. The last time I wrote a 'marriage in jeopardy' story I found it to be an incredibly challenging task, and this book was no different. Why? Because I was dealing with two characters with a shared and emotional history together, and I wanted to find a way for them to fall in love all over again. That meant dealing with their painful past, allowing them to forgive, and then creating a way for them to have a happy-ever-after as husband and wife.

In this story Luke Brown is a successful military man, capable of doing whatever it takes to complete a mission. But at home he struggles with being the husband he wants to be and the father that he knows his son deserves. The only thing he's sure about is that he'd do anything to turn back time and try to make things work with his wife, to be in his son's life... All he has to do is prove it to the woman he left behind two years earlier.

MISSION: SOLDIER TO DADDY is part of my *Heroes Come Home* series, and if you've missed any of my military-themed books be sure to visit my website for details on where to find them: www.sorayalane.com

Soraya

MISSION: SOLDIER TO DADDY

BY
SORAYA LANE

First published in Great Britain 2013
by Mills & Boon, an imprint of Harlequin (UK) Limited.
Harlequin (UK) Limited, Eton House, 18-24 Paradise Road,
Richmond, Surrey TW9 1SR

© Soraya Lane 2013

ISBN: 978 0 263 23439 8

Harlequin (UK) policy is to use papers that are natural, renewable
and r̶   le
forest
legal

Print
by Cl

Writing for Mills & Boon® is truly a dream come true for **Soraya Lane**. An avid reader and writer since her childhood, Soraya describes becoming a published author as 'the best job in the world' and hopes to be writing heart-warming, emotional romances for many years to come.

Soraya lives with her own real-life hero on a small farm in New Zealand, surrounded by animals and with an office overlooking a field where their horses graze.

For more information about Soraya and her upcoming releases visit her at her website, www.sorayalane.com, her blog, www.sorayalane.blogspot.com, or follow her at www.facebook.com/SorayaLaneAuthor

Recent books by Soraya Lane:

THE NAVY SEAL'S BRIDE
BACK IN THE SOLDIER'S ARMS
RODEO DADDY
THE ARMY RANGER'S RETURN
SOLDIER ON HER DOORSTEP

Did you know these are also available as eBooks?
Visit www.millsandboon.co.uk

Other titles by Soraya Lane available in eBook format.

For Hamish

CHAPTER ONE

A BUTTERFLY-SOFT SHIVER ran down Olivia Brown's spine. After all this time, she was scared of seeing her husband again. Scared of being confronted with the reality of the man who'd left her, and scared of how their son would react. Had she been right not to meet him at the airport?

"Is it almost time, Mommy?"

Olivia looked over at her son. His ruffled blond locks and paint-stained fingers tugged something inside her, and the worry started to knot in her stomach again.

"Not long now, honey. He'll be here soon."

She moved over to sit with her son, and squeezed his hand.

"Will I like him?"

"Your dad? Of course! You'll love him, Charlie."

Her boy nodded and twisted his mouth into a smile. "Will he like me?"

Olivia laughed and gave him a playful punch on the arm. "Have you ever met anyone who didn't adore you?"

Charlie jumped up then, his eyes wide. "Did you hear that?"

Olivia's eyes fluttered shut for a heartbeat. Yes, she'd heard it, and if it wasn't for her son she might just have fled the scene. When her eyes opened again, she was sitting at the table alone. The Welcome Home Daddy poster lay spread out in front of her, splotches of paint and glitter a blur to her eyes.

This was it.

In less than thirty seconds, if the slam of a car door was anything to go by, her husband would be stepping back into her life. Would be seeing his son for the first time in two years.

"He's here!"

Charlie's excited squeal pulled her out of her daydream and she squared her shoulders, determined to stay strong. There was a knock at the door. She moved out into the hallway just as Charlie lunged forward to open it.

Lieutenant Colonel Luke Brown was officially back home.

Olivia watched Charlie tugging open the door, and wiped her palms over her denim jeans. She might not be looking forward to this, but her son sure was.

Charlie was frozen as he looked at the man on the other side of the threshold. The one who'd smiled at them from the fridge these past two years. The one in the photo that Charlie kissed every night before bed. Well, the man himself was standing right on their doorstep, all tanned, toned and handsome, just like he'd always been. Only this time he was in uniform, the starched trousers and jacket hugging his frame.

There was no mistaking it was him, though. His blond hair was cropped short, skin golden as if he'd spent a week on an island. His dark brown eyes—eyes she could never forget even if she tried—staring straight back at her. He stood tall, uncomfortable almost, in his immaculate uniform.

"Daddy!"

Charlie's delayed yet exuberant outburst broke their stare. Olivia dropped her gaze and watched as her son saw his dad for the first time. Watched as he clutched on to the crisply pressed trousers as if he'd never let go.

"Charlie?" He hated that it was a question.

Luke counted to five in his mind, trying to stop from grabbing his little boy and squeezing the lifeblood from him. He'd waited for this moment for so long, and now this child, with hair the same blond as his own, stood before him, waiting expectantly as if his father would know what to do, when the truth was he had *no idea* how to even greet him. But he was back now and that's what counted.

Before he could drop his pack to the ground the tiny body hurtled forward, grabbing him tight around the legs. Luke barely had time to lock eyes with Ollie again, to see the reaction on her face, before he was thrown headfirst into fatherhood.

"I see you're not shy, huh?" He recovered from the tackle enough to straighten, bag dropped to the ground, one hand on his son's head. "Thought you'd be big enough for a handshake by now."

Charlie jumped back, saluting his dad, a grin plastered on his face. Luke responded in kind, straight-faced, at his boy pretending to be a soldier.

"You've been taking good care of the little soldier, huh?" Luke turned his attention back to his wife.

Olivia stood in the hall, her slender body braced by the wall. His eyes flicked over her, at the long honey-brown hair falling over her shoulders, at the slim arms crossed over her chest, and the sad blue eyes staring back at him. He hated seeing her like that. Knowing he was responsible for the sadness in her gaze.

"Aagghh! The poster!" Charlie spun around and motored down the hall past his mom, disappearing from sight. Luke watched for a moment, then stepped inside and closed the door behind him.

"How are you, Ollie?"

He stood at ease, feet spread evenly. His hands slipped into his pockets as he watched her—watched those beautiful, big blue eyes that were looking straight back at him.

"It's good to have you back, Luke."

Olivia's voice was strained. He tried to ignore it, but it hit him hard. He had imagined this day for a long time, thought about what he'd say and how he'd apologize to her. But now that he was here, expressing himself wasn't coming as easily as he'd hoped.

"It's good to be home." Should he close the distance between them and kiss her? Hug her and say "sorry"? He almost made himself laugh. What would he pick to say sorry for? Leaving her when he'd promised to stay? His royal failure at being a husband, or for being the world's worst father?

"He's been so excited about seeing you." Olivia gestured with her head as a thunder of footfalls echoed their way. "He hardly slept a wink all night."

Luke understood. How could he not? His son was excited to have him home, his wife wasn't. He didn't deserve anything more, but it still hurt.

"He's sure turned into a pretty special kid."

"Welcome home!" Charlie stood at his mom's side, arms stretched wide with the homemade poster. Luke looked at Olivia first, then at Charlie, and he wished things could have been different. That he'd been away a few months, maybe six. That he was coming home to a real family, to a wife who loved him still. The kind of family he had wished for over and over when he was a child.

"I love it," he said, dropping to his knees to inspect the picture. "You did great, kid."

His son beamed and grabbed his hand, tugging him in the direction he'd come from. "Come on, Dad."

Luke looked over his shoulder at Ollie and almost wished he'd stayed away. This was harder than he'd expected, and then some. He'd come home to see his son, but looking at his wife, he was wishing he'd made more of an effort in that department, too. More than an effort, he wished he'd taken the time to make things *right*.

When Luke looked back at her, gave her that soft smile he used to throw her way so often, Olivia almost broke down, but she was determined not to cry. She had to be strong for their son. It was all that mattered right now.

After all this time, of wishing Luke would come home, to almost wishing he'd never come back into their lives again, he was here. And she had to deal with it.

Those first few months had been the hardest, but then she'd become used to not having her husband around. She'd met other moms, new friends, fitted in in a way she hadn't thought possible. Developed a new life, like a widow. And regretted all the times she'd raised her voice at her husband, when she should have tried listening to him instead.

She'd well and truly prepared for the fact that he might never come home. *Until now.* His dedication to the army was something to be proud of, but the way he'd hurt her wasn't.

Olivia walked bravely into the living room and watched her son, rabbiting on to his father and dumping toys all over the ground as if he was playing show-and-tell. Luke had taken his jacket off and lay spread out on the floor, his uniformed legs eating up the carpet, white undershirt a contrast to the charcoal weave.

She ached to reach out and touch him, no matter how

much she hated herself for thinking that, but he was just so damn gorgeous. *So handsome,* and the memories she had of him were so good. It was as if she needed to make contact with his skin to prove that he was here. *Alive.* In their house.

But reuniting with Luke wasn't a possibility. The thrum of hurt still ached like a constant thud, and having him back only made the pain more real. She couldn't do it again. Not now. She'd finally rebuilt her life, and if she lost him again she'd never recover.

The divorce papers were in her bag; she just had to decide when to tell him. She was sure he'd given up on their marriage long before she had, so now it was just time to make it official.

"Okay, time to let me talk to your mom, okay?" she heard him tell Charlie.

Olivia turned to see Luke pull his big frame up to full height.

"Coffee?" she asked, busying herself in the kitchen for something to do.

He nodded and sat down across from her. She sensed him watching her as she dropped instant coffee into each cup. Scooped sugar into her mug, then refilled the dispenser—anything to avoid his gaze.

"Nice place here."

Olivia paused and looked at him. "I had to move. It just wasn't practical to stay in the old house." Her voice had a bite to it. A snap she hadn't intended.

Luke raised his hands. "I didn't mean anything by it. You don't have to explain."

Heat hit her cheeks and she turned to pour boiling water into each cup. Of course he hadn't meant anything by it. She was just jittery and jumping to conclusions.

"Luke, I…" She placed the mug in front of him and tried to find the words.

He reached out to her, catching her wrist as she let one hand rest on the counter. The simple press of his skin against hers made her pull away, recoil. But it also made her flush with something other than anger. Because she still wanted Luke, no matter how much she tried to make herself think otherwise.

"You don't have to say anything. This is hard for me, too, Ollie."

No! she wanted to scream at him. *You have no idea how I feel, no idea how lonely I've been, how some nights I just wished you were dead, so I could move on with my life.*

There had been times when she'd almost wished the worst would happen to him, even though the guilt of her thoughts would later eat away at her. But the way things had ended between them, the regrets she had for what she'd said and done, the pain from his actions, had pushed her to the edge.

She stood and sipped her coffee, hand shaking ever so slightly. Luke did the same, but he didn't look back at her. Instead he stared into the black liquid, eyes down. She hoped he couldn't read her thoughts.

"Mommy?"

Charlie's voice pulled her back to reality. A welcome relief to the strained feeling between her and Luke.

"Can we go outside?"

She glanced at Luke and he nodded, taking a few quick sips of his drink before standing. Charlie looked innocent, his head on a slight angle as if he wasn't sure what was happening.

"Let's go kick a ball or something, huh?" Luke suggested.

Ollie watched as he took Charlie's hand. Watched as they walked from the room and out the door, father and son.

Luke was all muscle—lean and toned. A bit on the thin side, but handsome and strong nonetheless. Her body still yearned for him, and so did her heart, but things were different now. He'd broken his promise and left her, and she could never forgive him for ending things. She had to protect herself and her son.

It wasn't that she didn't believe in patriotism. She did. But she also believed in family. A soldier didn't just walk out on his family, no matter what. Not like Luke had. Could she ever trust him not to leave Charlie again?

"He's out cold."

Luke sat back down at the table and poured himself another glass of wine. He hadn't drunk more than the odd beer in years, but this was at least helping him deal with being back.

Ollie looked up at him, and he resisted the urge to reach out. To touch her and remember what things had once been like for them. He knew it was a lot to expect, her having him here, but it wasn't as if they were pretending to be together again. Except maybe just a little, to keep things uncomplicated for their son.

"Why didn't you call, Luke?"

If he could have hung his head any lower, he would have. He'd been a lousy husband and an even worse dad, and he had no excuse. But her question still made him feel like dirt. Luke took another sip of wine and stared back at her.

"We were lucky to hear from you every other month."

He frowned. "It was hard to make contact." He knew it sounded phony, and the truth was he should have made more of an effort, but…damn it! He knew he'd stuffed up, and it wasn't something he'd wanted to do.

"Bull!" She stood with a thump, glaring at him as she swore. "Don't lie to me, Luke. You had a little boy here who cried for his daddy night after night, and you couldn't make the effort to call more? He's had to grow up without even remembering or knowing who you were."

Luke stayed seated. He was not going to argue with her. Not on his first night home. Not like they used to. But at one point, when he had been at his lowest, that's what he'd wanted: for Charlie to forget him so he never knew the pain of loss.

"Keep your voice down, Ollie. You'll wake Charlie," he said.

"How dare you!" she growled. "I've kept my voice down every night, doing nothing *but* look after our son. He's been my life, Luke. While you've been off fighting for our country, I've been fighting for our son. For me. For our family." She paused and glared at him, her voice dropping an octave. "While you decided not to give a damn."

Her eyes were full of tears. Luke looked away. He couldn't watch her. Couldn't bear to see the sadness, the emptiness in her eyes. Worst of all, he knew she was right.

"I know it's been hard for you…."

The silence that stretched between them seemed to drain the air of oxygen. But it wasn't just his fault, was it? Ollie hadn't exactly acted as if she'd wanted him to stay, and he'd never forgotten it.

"You have *no idea* how hard it's been, Luke. Don't even try to understand. I was here alone, with a little boy who deserved a father." Her voice cracked. "It wasn't that you left me, it was that you left our son."

Luke stood and walked into the kitchen. He couldn't hide behind the excuse of being a soldier any longer, and

Ollie was right. His son didn't deserve to grow up without a dad, and he knew firsthand why. Because it was how he'd grown up, and he'd come home to make sure history didn't repeat itself, that his son knew him.

"Olivia, I'm sorry. I am."

"You forget that I've been around army wives for the last two years." Olivia was standing behind him in the kitchen now, her voice still laced with tears. "They had calls at least every month, once a week even, and their husbands took leave and came home, even if it was only a few days. With your rank… Oh, I don't even know anymore, Luke. But I do know that you could have done more."

He looked back at his wife, ashamed. Walking out had been the easy option for him when things had become difficult, and he'd taken it. When their son had refused to sleep, when his wife had never believed he would have married her unless she was pregnant, knowing that he could die on deployment and leave his boy without a dad, just as he'd experienced…

"It was too hard to talk to you, Ollie. Charlie, too. It was easier not to." It was a struggle to push the words out, to make himself be honest with her. "You have no idea how many times I picked up a phone, how many times I wanted to talk to you and couldn't go through with it."

"Yeah, well, maybe you should have."

By the time he looked back up, she was gone.

Luke dropped his head into his hands, eyes shut. Maybe if they hadn't gotten pregnant so soon, if they hadn't rushed into marriage, things would have been different. Maybe they never would have married at all. But all that mattered right now was making it up to his son, and proving to him that he was here for him, that he was committed to being his dad.

Because this time he had no intention of walking away.

CHAPTER TWO

CHARLIE'S HEAD APPEARED next to the bed and Luke squinted at the bedside clock. It was 2:00 a.m.

"Hey, buddy." He reached out a hand and touched Charlie's head. Luke didn't know what else to do. He'd never really been around kids, *not even his own.*

His son blinked at him, big brown eyes peering down at him as the little boy leaned closer.

"Can I get into bed with you?" Charlie whispered.

"Uh, yeah, I guess."

Luke pulled the covers back. He hated that he didn't know what to do. Should he send him back to his own bed? Cuddle him? What?

Now Charlie was snuggling hard against him, and Luke knew there was no going back. He put his arm out, feeling awkward. Not sure what to say, to his own son.

"Daddy?"

Luke swallowed. *Daddy.* It was a name he'd dreamed of being called for two long years, but now he didn't know how to even be a dad. When he'd left, Charlie had been so young, and now Luke could see how much he'd missed out on. "Yes, Charlie?"

"I love you."

"Well, uh, I love you, too." Luke choked. He tried to

swallow again. Thank God it was dark and his son couldn't see him.

"You won't go away again, will you, Daddy?"

"No, bud." He held his son close, fighting back tears. Truth was, he didn't know when he'd be going away again, but he wasn't going to let his son know that. It was what he did—the army called and he had to jump to attention. He'd tried to think otherwise sometimes, that maybe he could change vocation, but being a soldier was what he did, and he did it damn well. He had a few months without having to leave, and then he didn't know what he was going to do. Or how he was going to leave things here.

"I like having a dad."

Great. Talk about pulling on his heartstrings. Luke pushed away the feelings he'd tried so long to keep hidden—the guilt of leaving his son and repeating the cycle. Of letting his own child go through what he'd been through, what he'd struggled with his whole life: growing up without a dad and wishing like hell his life could have been different. But then, deep down, he'd rather Charlie not even know his dad than lose him and remember what he'd lost for the rest of his life. Like he had.

He'd gone all these years in the army without crying, and now he was on the verge of turning into a blubbering baby.

"Will you ever sleep in Mom's bed?"

That made him smile. "Let's hope so, kiddo."

He knew it was a lie, a fib at a stretch. Ollie was never going to let him back in her bed, and although it was tempting to think about being under the sheets with her, that wasn't why he was here. He'd come home for his son, to get to know the boy, not with any illusions that Ollie would take him back. Things had been strained between them, and he'd helped their marriage go from bad to worse.

"Do you have a night-light?"

Had someone taught his son interrogation techniques? "Let's get some sleep, huh?"

Luke snuggled him even closer, tucking his son's little body into his.

Maybe he *could* do this whole dad routine. He only wished he could have gotten a handle on the husband part, too.

Ollie pressed against the door and tried to ignore the tears leaving a wet trail down her cheeks. She should have walked away as soon as she'd heard Charlie talking to his dad, but instead she'd stood and listened.

She'd risen, so in tune with her son and used to him getting up in the night. Part of her loved that he'd gone in to see his dad, but part of her hated it, too—that for the first time he'd gone to someone else instead of climbing into bed with her. They'd had over two years together, she and Charlie, just the two of them, and changing that was hard.

Ollie walked silently back down to her room and crawled into bed. But those words kept playing over and over in her mind. *Will you ever sleep in Mommy's bed?* The man who'd driven her crazy, made her fall so in love with him after such a short time together, and now they were like strangers. Would he have ever come back if it wasn't for Charlie? Would she have deserved it? Because no matter what she said or felt, part of the blame in their marriage breaking down was her doing. And it was time she admitted it.

Ollie squeezed her eyes shut and tried to find sleep, but she had a feeling that slumber wasn't going to be quite that simple. Kind of like her marriage.

* * *

The noise in the living room woke Ollie before she was ready to open her eyes. What was going on out there?

She rose, checked the drawstring on her pajama bottoms and pulled her tank top into line.

"Mommy!"

Charlie charged her, just about taking her pants down with her as he tugged her along. The remnants of a train track were sprawled in every direction. Railcars and engines added to the carnage.

"Morning."

She looked up from the train wreck and into the kitchen. Luke stood there bare-chested, in just his boxer shorts. She took in a deep breath and self-consciously ran a hand through her bed hair. *Damn.* Taut, tanned torso, a sprinkling of hair on his chest that arrowed down into his shorts… She'd forgotten how good he looked without his clothes on.

Ollie ran her focus up his body again and met twinkling eyes. She quickly diverted her gaze.

"Breakfast?" He gestured with his head and she took a step forward to peer into the kitchen.

"He's making pancakes, Mom. Pancakes!"

Charlie scooted up to Luke and hung off him as if they were glued together, not shy of his dad at all.

"Your favorite, huh?"

He grinned. "How many you going to have, Mom?"

She gave her son a smile before meeting Luke's gaze. Ollie knew how dreadful she probably looked, all mussed from bed. When they'd first met she'd worn sexy teddies, not gingham pj's.

"I'm just going to jump in the shower. Save me a couple, okay, Charlie?"

She directed her words to him to avoid conversation

with Luke, but doubted her son had even heard her. He was yabbering away to his dad a hundred miles a minute, and Luke was flipping pancakes to exuberant yelps of excitement.

Ollie left the room and flopped down onto her bed, exhausted already. She'd hardly slept a wink and now her stranger husband was making breakfast for their son, and she had no idea what to do. What her role even was right now.

She knew the reality was that the man she'd married had been a soldier, and going away had been part of the deal, but he'd swept her off her feet and made her forget all that. Until she'd gotten pregnant and he'd proposed, and everything had slowly started to unravel. Because she'd never truly believed that he would have married her otherwise, and because the night before she'd found out she actually was pregnant, Luke had told her that he never, ever wanted to be a dad.

Luke's dedication to the army had seemed so exciting when she'd first met him. But doubt had gnawed at her for so many months, and then with a difficult baby and no one to help her through the tough times, she'd snapped. More than once. And eventually, Luke had walked out the door and never come back.

"What do you say we head to the park?"

She watched Luke smile at Charlie as he leaped up, jumping around, no doubt hyper from all the sugar in their breakfast.

"I'm not sure," said Ollie. "I've got to get to work."

She sighed. Her husband and son looked up at her like sad puppies.

"What do you usually do with Charlie?" Luke asked.

Ollie scooped up their coffee mugs and sticky maple-syrup-covered plates and took them into the kitchen. "He comes to work with me. Ricardo's pretty relaxed about Charlie tagging along."

"Ricardo?" Luke's attention was suddenly focused directly on her, eyes as sharp as a hawk's.

"My boss. Ricardo Bolton." She paused and leaned back on the counter. "He's an attorney. I clean his place, have dinner in the fridge for him, all the general housekeeping type stuff so he can focus on work, and he doesn't mind if Charlie tags along with me."

"Right."

It seemed so weird, having this type of conversation with her husband. Ricardo had become a close friend, but the way Luke was looking at her made her wonder if he thought their relationship was something else.

"And does this Ricardo man know you're still married?"

Ollie laughed. *She* hardly remembered she was married sometimes, given her lack of husband.

"He likes Mom," chirped Charlie, dragging his dad by the hand to reinspect his train set.

Luke picked the boy up, but his attention was still focused on her.

"It's nothing like that," she said, but her cheeks heated, giving her away. She'd always been a terrible liar. Her son had meant nothing by it, couldn't have meant anything by it, but the implication was obvious. And for some stupid reason she felt guilty about it.

"What about your drawing? You were still doing some illustrating before I left."

"Ricardo's a great employer and we needed the extra money. No time to waste on dreams anymore," she told him.

Ollie smiled at Luke before turning to the dishes. She felt no attraction whatsoever to Ricardo, but he was always making it clear that he'd like her to be more than just the housekeeper. Something she had no intention of ever agreeing to, but at least he made her feel wanted.

"Maybe I'll take Charlie to the park while you go to work," Luke suggested.

She nodded, but Luke had already turned away, his attention back on the toy box that Charlie was enthusiastically tipping upside down, to better show his dad what was inside.

Part of her, just a tiny part, wished that her husband had walked in their door and made the same sort of fuss over her as he was over his son. That they could start over, have fun again. But in her heart, she knew it was over. For good.

CHAPTER THREE

Luke looked across the dinner table, trying to figure out how to say what had to be said. He'd already been here a day, and the longer he took to talk to his wife, the harder it was going to get. Charlie was in bed, so it was now or never. He might not have come home with the intention of righting his marriage, but now that he was here it was all he could think about.

"Ollie, I need to get a few things off my chest."

She placed her knife and fork neatly on the plate before looking up, her gaze fixed on him.

"What you said yesterday was right. I should have called more, made more of an effort. All I can say is that I'm sorry." He paused. "I'm just not good at this sort of thing."

The silence between them was painful.

"What makes you think I am?" Ollie asked, looking down then back up at him. "It wasn't like I was great at talking *or* listening before you left."

Luke didn't know what to say. He watched her, his wife, and wondered how things had gotten to this point. How he'd let her slip away. She was the best thing that had ever happened to him, and instead of admitting that he'd run like a scared rabbit, because it had been easier than dealing with whatever had been going on with them. "Is there any way we can make this work, for Charlie's sake?"

Ollie just stared at him, her mouth pursed, eyebrows forming an angry frown. He'd expected to take her by surprise, but he hadn't expected that look.

Besides, he'd said the wrong thing. It wasn't just for Charlie's sake, it was because he still loved her, and instead of telling her that he'd managed to insult her.

Luke wanted to hold her, talk to her, listen to what she had to say, as he used to do. But it was as if there was nothing left between them, and asking for a second chance wasn't something he knew how to do.

"I'm sorry," he said.

"Sorry's not good enough, Luke."

Ollie wanted to hit him, curse at him, yell—but she couldn't. *Fight,* that's what she wanted. To fight him, argue, get it all out, but she didn't want to go down that path again, because if she thought of the months before Luke had gone, the weeks right before he'd left, that's all she could remember. Picking fights, wanting to punish him somehow for telling her he didn't want to be a dad, instead of making him open up to her and explain why.

Their marriage was over; she knew that. But it was time they discussed their problems like the adults they were, instead of the young kids they'd been when they'd married.

"Charlie needs both his parents, Luke, but us being together isn't a reality."

Luke watched her, giving nothing away. Then he sighed. "I know."

Give him a star for trying, but even he knew there was no hope. She knew if he was serious about them he would have acted on it sooner. Would have made more of an effort and not let it get to this point. Wouldn't have walked away in the first place, or would have at least come back before now.

"You walked out on our marriage, Luke. I know I was partly to blame, but I would never, ever have walked away from you."

He nodded, palms flat on the table, his foot tapping insistently on the floor as if he wanted to get up and walk away right now.

"Luke…" She paused, not sure how to say what she needed to tell him. "Luke, I just don't know if I could love you anymore." There, she'd said it. Said the words that had been choking her for weeks, months, years even. A weight lifted like a veil that had been suffocating her. Because what had happened between them had changed everything.

"I understand." His voice was deep. Full of emotion. "Of course I understand."

She paused again, pushing her fears back down her throat, sucking back the tears. "Then what are we doing here? Why are we pretending that it's okay you're back here staying with us?" Ollie stood up and paused at the window. Touched her head to the cool of the glass.

She felt rather than heard him rise. He was standing behind her. Every hair on her body stood at attention, aware of him being so close. Too close.

"We're married, Ollie. We have a son. That does still mean something."

Ollie turned, her eyes locking hard on to his. She knew it meant *something,* but he couldn't just walk back into their lives and expect her to fall in a heap at his feet. She had to protect her own heart, and her son's. It wasn't just about her and Luke anymore. It hadn't been since Charlie had been born.

"Those things aren't enough to make us work. To make *this* work. We need to be good parents, nothing more.

What we had has gone, and we don't need to stay married for Charlie to be happy."

Tears flowed freely down her cheeks. She acknowledged their cold, wet presence and didn't try to stop them.

"I don't want him growing up without a family." Luke punched out the words. "Because then I'd be putting him through what I went through, and I can't live with that."

"Neither do I," she snapped back, unable to hide how angry she was. Luke had made it obvious that she had nothing to do with why he wanted to possibly stay married, but was it just because he didn't want to repeat his own past, or something more? "Do you really think we could be together again, after all this time of growing apart?"

He shrugged, a noncommittal movement of the shoulders that told her nothing.

"You left me, *alone,* all that time, and I don't think I'll ever get over that."

"Now you're being unreasonable!" he bellowed, his soft demeanor disappearing quicker than it had arrived. "*I had no choice.* You knew my duty when you married me, and things were already bad well before I left." He shook his head. "When I called and heard your voice on the phone, when I rang and then had to hang up as soon as you answered, I didn't know where to start, or what I could say."

"You said you'd leave the army for me, Luke." She wasn't ready to admit that their marriage had already been teetering too close to the edge before she'd found out he was leaving. Or to acknowledge the fact that he *had* tried to call her more often than he had. "You promised. And then you walked out on our marriage like it meant nothing to you."

"I had to go, Ollie. Leaving my boys over there would have been wrong and you know it." His voice went soft, low. "But what I did to you, leaving, was unforgivable and not a day has gone past that I haven't wished things could have been different."

She knew her last comment had been a low blow; she shouldn't have said it. But it was what she had held so close for so long. Thought about when she'd lain awake at night, alone, with no husband next to her in the bed. When they'd hit a rough patch he'd taken the easy option and just left, when all she'd wanted was for him to fight for her. No matter what had happened, how hard things had been, all she'd wished for was that he could prove to her that he'd married her for more than just the sake of her being pregnant. That she wasn't being used by men like her mom had been.

"I can't do this again, Luke. We can't make this work."

She'd only just got over him. Just managed to move on, and now he was asking for what? A second chance? Was he just trying to make sure she'd let him see his son? Because she'd never stop him from being in Charlie's life.

Luke strode the two steps to stand before her, to tower over her small frame. *"No."*

"No?"

"You heard me." His voice was determined now, commanding rather than questioning. "I did my duty, served my country. The way I left you makes me a crappy husband, but it doesn't mean I don't deserve a chance to at least be a better dad, Ollie."

Ollie stayed silent. She didn't trust her voice. She should have been grateful that it was his son he wanted, but a little voice cried out in her mind, because it would have felt so good to know he wanted her, too. To hear him say he'd do anything to be back in *her* life again.

"I want to be there for Charlie."

"But, Luke…" Her voice cracked as he reached out one hand to steady her shaking arm.

Her voice was barely a whisper when she finally spoke again. "I can't put us in a position to be left again. You need to prove yourself to me, Luke, and to Charlie, before you can be his full-time dad. Right now you're like a new toy, but how long before the batteries fail and you're gone again?"

She held his gaze, kept her chin high. She was *not* going to allow her heart to be broken again. This was it, and she couldn't take a chance on trusting him when she didn't know how long he'd be here, and how long he'd be gone next time. It had been too easy for him to leave, and now he'd come back to them, hoping to start again.

"I want a divorce, Luke." The words were hard to say, but she had to tell him. Because if she didn't she'd be kidding herself *and him.*

"A divorce?" He stepped back as if she'd hit him.

"I'm sorry," she sobbed, tears making it hard to speak as she walked away. "I just can't do this. Not again. What we had didn't work, Luke, and we both need to understand that."

All Olivia had ever wanted was a family of her own, a husband who loved her, but that fantasy was past its use-by date. It was just her and Charlie, and she couldn't let Luke thunder back into their lives like a tornado. Charlie needed a father who hung around, or was at least a whole lot better at staying in touch when he wasn't.

"Olivia."

She heard Luke say her name, but she didn't want to turn around.

"Olivia, please."

But there were no words he could say right now to change how she felt.

CHAPTER FOUR

OLLIE'S CHEEKS HURT. She could hear her own laughter echoing around them as Luke twirled her, over and over again.

"Stop!"

He drew her in, hard against him, his muscled body tight against hers.

"Say you love me."

"Luke, let go of me!" She squirmed in his arms.

"Say it, baby, or I'll toss you in the water."

He lifted her off her feet so only her toes trailed on the sand, and started walking her toward the ocean.

"I love you, I love you!" she cried, her arms around his neck.

"Too late."

She started to tell him off, to swat at him, but he dropped her into the water, diving in himself. Her hair was plastered to her face, mascara dripped into her eyes, but she still couldn't stop smiling.

He resurfaced. "Come here often?"

Luke lay next to her, half floating on his stomach, and pushed his hair off his face. Water fell from his dark lashes, and she felt herself fall apart. Those brown eyes looked straight through her, past her insecurities and worries, straight into her heart.

"Look what you've done to me." She giggled, rubbing beneath her eyes. "I'm a mess."

"You," he said, kissing her nose, "are—" another kiss "—not a mess."

She kissed him back then, their wet lips pressed together, her hands in his hair.

"I do love you, Luke."

"I know, honey, I know."

Ollie woke with a fright. *It was just a dream.* She wanted to cry, sob her heart out, because here she was, dreaming about the man she'd fallen head over heels in love with, the only man she'd ever loved, who was so close yet so far away. Her own husband, in the spare room, so near that she could wake him just by thudding on the wall. But not the same man he'd been back then.

Her heart stilled, but she was rattled. It was always the same dream. The day she'd gotten pregnant, the one time they hadn't used protection. The same day she'd decided that Luke was the man of her dreams, before everything had slowly started to unravel.

A gentle tap made her stare at the door. Charlie would never knock; he would just come marching on in.

Ollie slipped out of bed and pulled on her robe, checking to see she had everything covered. She took a deep breath before opening the door.

"Hey." It was Luke. Who else had she expected?

"Hey," she whispered back.

She didn't know if it was the dream or just the time of night, but she couldn't take her eyes from his face. His hair, his lips, the stubble on his jaw. Just like he used to look. *Yet somehow even better.*

"Are you okay?" he asked.

Her eyebrows knotted. Why wouldn't she be okay? It was the middle of the night. "Ah, sure, I'm fine."

Luke looked uncomfortable. "It's just, I heard you calling out. Must have been a dream."

This time it was Ollie who was uncomfortable. Her stomach churned as if she'd eaten something bad. "Mmm," she mumbled, "must have."

"Okay, well, I'll, uh, head back to bed then."

Ollie watched him, her embarrassment starting to fade. There had been a time when she would have told Luke anything, had thought they would be in love and happy forever. And looking at him now, she almost felt they *had* gone back. Gone back to when they were dating, to the early days of her pregnancy, before they'd realized that maybe they'd rushed into marriage, that things weren't so easy with a newborn baby. That they hadn't talked through their pasts or their problems enough, before making such a massive commitment to one another.

She took in the pajama bottoms, the bare chest, the trail of hair that skewered from his belly button as he turned back to face her. He was standing there, just looking at her, not moving.

"Ollie…" His voice trailed off.

"Yes?" She waited expectantly, desperate for him to say something, *anything*.

His swift movement took her by surprise. She gasped, eyes locked on his as he pulled her tight against him, pressed his lips hard onto hers. She knew she was rigid, fought it, but as she softened into him, melted into his arms, he, too, softened the kiss. Moved his lips over hers so delicately that she thought her legs would buckle.

It was over too quick. He pulled away and took a step back, his eyes tracing her face, looking for an answer.

"I never stopped thinking about you, Ollie," he said,

his voice low and husky. "I never, ever stopped wondering how the hell things had gone so wrong. How I'd managed to wreck what we had, and wished we could just go back in time."

She stood there, mute, hand raised to her lips. What could she say to that? He'd sure had a bad way of showing how he felt.

"Luke, I…"

"No." He said the word firmly. "Don't say anything. Just promise you won't give up on us, not yet. Let's give it one more go. I might not deserve it, but let me try to make it up to you, Ollie."

Olivia stayed still. She didn't know what to say, anyway. She loved the memory of him, loved the look of the man standing in front of her, but she didn't know if she *actually* loved him now or not. Didn't know if she could ever truly forgive him, or trust him not to leave her. Did he still want *her,* or was it just for Charlie's sake that he wanted to try again?

"I'm going to make you trust me, but first you have to say you'll give me a chance."

"Luke, I already have the divorce papers."

"Give me a month, Ollie, or two. After that, I'll sign the papers." The look on his face told her he was being honest, that he genuinely believed it was worth trying. "I've had a lot of time to think, and I know things ended badly between us, but we're married and we have a son. That counts for something. I know it and you know it."

She bit down on her bottom lip, eyes on him. He was staring at her with that deep, brooding look. The sort of look she hadn't seen on his face other than the day Charlie had been born.

"There's something about being back here that makes me think we could be a family. For real."

"You will actually be here for a whole month?" she asked.

He'd never said how long he was back for, never said when he'd be needed again. She didn't know anything other than he was "off duty" for a while.

Luke just stared at her, unblinking. "I promise I'm here for a while. I haven't signed up for anything else yet, and I'm owed a decent amount of time off."

Could she do it? Actually put her heart on the line and give him a second chance? Believe what he was telling her? Change her mind and actually say *yes* to him?

"So what do you say?" Luke asked.

"Okay," she whispered. Only because she wanted to see if he *could* change her mind.

"One month?" he asked.

As long as it takes. "Let's just see how we go," she answered.

Luke backed away from her, edging slowly down the hall. She was planted on the spot, her feet powerless to walk away even if she'd wanted to. What she would give to have pulled him into her room, to have made love to him just like they'd had crazy, passionate sex on the beach in her dream.

But he was right. Maybe they did have to give it a chance, for Charlie's sake. But he was going to have to prove to her that he deserved a second chance before she ever let him back in. It had been so long, and she knew he was probably full of conflict from his time abroad. He could just as easily take flight and leave her all over again, and this time he would leave a heartbroken kid behind, too.

She was strong, so she could see him leave now and force a wall over her heart. But Charlie couldn't. Her boy would be affected forever if he fell in love with his dad and then he left, but she didn't have any control over that.

She could stop Luke from affecting *her,* but he had rights to his son, and she wasn't going to stand in his way. Yet.

Luke tried his hardest not to look back over his shoulder. He balled one fist as he walked, turning into his room as if he was marching. His body rigid.

He had come home with no intention of a reconcili-ation—no intention of asking for Ollie back. What he'd wanted was to be there for his son. But being home, spending time with his boy and being around his wife was driving him crazy. His perfect little family was still within his grasp, and he had to grab hold as quickly as he could to avoid losing them. Forever.

He'd never stopped regretting leaving them the first time, but they'd all been so young. Charlie had been so difficult, and Ollie had seemed determined to push Luke away. He'd panicked over being a dad, struggled for so long without being able to talk to his wife about it without her exploding, and then he'd joined his unit and never come home. Been promoted to a Special Operations task force and tried not to look back.

But right now he had a chance, and he wasn't going to walk away again without trying. All his life he'd been told he wasn't good enough, had grown up thinking he didn't deserve a family, that there was a reason he'd been left, that the way he'd been treated in foster care was normal. But he had a chance now to right the wrongs he'd made, to give his son the kind of home he'd wanted so bad as a kid, and to make things right with his wife. To stop being afraid of *what if* and live in the now.

All he needed to do was figure out *how.*

Ollie kept her hands busy with dinner and her ears on Luke. It wasn't an easy conversation to be having, she'd give him that, but he owed it to Charlie to be straight with him. And if Luke hadn't told him, then it would have been left to her—again.

"I know I said I wouldn't leave you, bud, but it's, well, it's tricky."

Charlie was pouting. He didn't throw tantrums often, but she was starting to think this could turn into one.

"But you said," he whined.

Now Ollie was sure they were moving into meltdown territory.

"Okay, I'll make you a promise," she heard Luke say.

Charlie jumped to attention then, his frown disappearing, but Ollie had one hover across her lips instead. The last thing she needed was to deal with a broken promise. She bit down on her lip, determined not to interfere.

"I promise that I'll tell you where I'm going and for how long, *if* I go away. And I'll phone you while I'm gone," Luke said.

Ollie pretended to toss the salad, and tried hard to keep her eyes down. Could he keep that promise?

"Really?" Charlie asked.

"Yep, really." Luke smiled and extended his hand. "Shake and it becomes a real promise. A *man's* promise."

Olivia dropped the serving spoon by mistake. A man's promise? She didn't know whether she should be hoping he'd be able to keep it, or annoyed that he'd even made it.

She turned to see Charlie slowly put his hand into his father's. *Trusting.* Trusting that he could believe in the big promise his father had just made him.

"See these soldiers?" asked Luke, holding them up for his son to see.

Charlie nodded.

"This one here is a sergeant." He reached out and placed it in his hand. "This fellow here, well, he's a private."

"What are you, Daddy?" Charlie's question made Ollie's breath catch in her throat.

"Well, son, I'm a lieutenant colonel, and that means I have to lead my men, to make sure that people like you and Mommy back here are safe. We have to go on special operations."

Charlie had started out listening to his dad, but now he was walking the soldier figurines around the carpet. But Olivia was listening. How could she not? Because no matter what had happened between them, she was incredibly proud of Luke's career.

Luke knew Ollie was watching. He'd known all along that she was listening, but he didn't mind. Part of this promise was about showing her that he was serious about being a dad, but it was a hell of a lot easier to talk to Charlie than to her. Most of all, he just wanted to be honest, and talking didn't come easy to him.

His men had always trusted him with their lives, but he knew that earning Olivia's trust would be hard. And he still hadn't told her the truth about where he'd been and what he had been doing. That he was part of a Special Forces task force, that he'd been immersed in another culture most of the time he'd been away. That he'd never been so terrified in his life, and that when he'd almost died, had come so close to becoming a casualty, all he'd thought of was her.

Luke left Charlie to his playing and joined Ollie in the kitchen. If he was serious about them giving this a real go, then he needed to make an effort. *A big effort.*

"So, uh, how are you feeling about last night?" Luke cringed at his words. *Idiot.* Not quite how he'd planned on saying it. Ollie's face now flushed a deep pink and he looked down at his feet. *He never had been very good at this whole talking business.*

He looked up and found her fussing with the food she was making, maybe finding this as awkward as he was.

"What's for dinner?" he asked next.

That at least elicited a smile in his direction.

"Oh, just lasagna with a salad. Nothing much."

"Just lasagna? Sounds like more than nothing to me."

"I've made dessert, too. Charlie's favorite."

Luke hated that he didn't know what his son liked to eat.

"Chocolate cake," Ollie said, as if knowing that he was floundering. "Slathered with icing and with a little ice cream on the side."

"Sounds like we have the same favorites."

They looked at one another. Luke couldn't drop his gaze. There was something there, he knew it, something that hadn't disappeared despite the time that had passed, despite the way things had ended between them. Olivia looked away first, but Luke couldn't. He kept watching her, wishing that he was one for talking, about his feelings, about what he wanted.

But last night he had, and now he had to prove himself to her, and as easy as it would be to run, to go back to the army, he was going to try his hardest. Not just for Charlie, but because of Olivia. His *wife*. No more excuses. This time he was going to prove himself and make her believe in him again, and he wasn't going to let her down.

Because maybe he did deserve it. Maybe he wasn't destined to fail at being a husband and a dad.

Maybe, just maybe, he could be successful at more than just being a soldier. And maybe he'd come home for Olivia as much as he'd come home for his son.

CHAPTER FIVE

THE COOL WIND made the tiny hairs on Olivia's arm rise in protest, but she ignored it. All she could think about was Luke, and no matter how hard she tried not to, it was impossible. Every month he'd been away she'd thought about him, so why had she expected it would be different, having him home? Perhaps without Charlie as a constant reminder, it might have been.

Olivia looked up as she reached her employer's apartment. It was weird arriving on her own, when for almost a year she'd made the walk with a little hand tucked into her own.

"Hello," she called as she let herself in, just in case Ricardo was home.

She was greeted by silence. Olivia shrugged off her coat and walked into the kitchen, dropping her belongings on the counter. The place was immaculate as usual, just like she'd left it, as if he hadn't even been home since the last time she'd visited.

Olivia crossed the room, heading for the fridge. She paused to read the note on the counter beside it: "I'd love that homemade pasta sauce for dinner tonight, darling! R."

Fresh pasta and her tomato and basil sauce. Perfect. Now she could just ponder her thoughts and prepare dinner, on autopilot.

And try again to stop thinking about Luke.

* * *

Luke stood at ease as he watched Charlie run around the playground. His son had zoomed down the slide over and over, and was now making a beeline for the jungle gym.

"Come on, Dad." Charlie waved excitedly for him to follow.

There were plenty of kids around, all doing their own thing, accompanied by their nannies or moms. Luke was the odd man out, but he didn't care. So long as no one realized he had no idea what he was doing, he'd be fine.

"Daddy! Daddy, look!"

Luke looked up in time to see Charlie hanging upside down, showing all his teeth he was smiling so hard. Luke gulped. This looked like a rescue mission to him.

"Stay still, bud. I'll get you." He gritted his teeth and jogged forward.

"Look, look! I'm upside down."

Luke was looking, just not with the enthusiasm his son seemed to expect. How the hell had Charlie managed to scramble so high? Did Olivia let him do this sort of thing, or was he supposed to stop him?

A manual. He definitely needed a manual.

Charlie wriggled back onto the bars, still grinning, then landed with a thud on both feet.

"What next?"

"As in where are we going next?" Luke asked. Was there somewhere else they were supposed to be going?

"No! What do we play on next?"

A noise from behind him made Luke turn.

"Hi there." The voice belonged to a pretty brunette.

"Uh, hi."

"I just wondered if you were new to the area? We haven't seen you here before."

Luke followed her nod, and saw that two other young moms were watching them.

"Yeah, new," he said. "Well, I lived near here for a while before I shipped out."

"So you're a soldier?" she asked.

Luke was flattered by the seduction in her voice, but he wasn't interested. And he wasn't exactly sure how to make that clear to her. "Yes, ma'am. Just arrived back from offshore."

She turned around and smiled at her friends. Luke took his chance to change the subject. He reached for Charlie's hand. His marriage might not be in the best shape right now, but his problems at being a husband had nothing to do with infidelity.

"I'm running a bit late to see my wife, so we'd best be off. Nice to meet you," he said.

The woman looked disappointed, but she didn't give up. "I'm Lisa." She thrust out her hand.

"Nice to meet you, Lisa," he said firmly. "Have a nice day."

Luke saw her frown before he turned, but he didn't care. A hand tugging his reminded him that he wasn't alone, and that he had better things to worry about than hurting a stranger's feelings. Especially one as forward as this woman.

"Who was that?" asked Charlie.

"Nobody we'll ever see again," said Luke, ruffling his boy's hair. "You want to have a go on the slide again before we leave?"

"Then we'll go see Mom?"

Of course. Charlie had heard him say they were off to see Olivia, so he thought that was where they were going.

"I don't actually know where she works," Luke admitted.

"I do!" shouted Charlie, taking him by surprise. "Let's go."

Luke had no choice but to comply, and he wasn't complaining. Being dragged around by an almost four-year-old had its benefits, and being lost in the moment was one of them.

Despite trusting that Charlie actually did have a sense of direction, and letting go of his own desire to be in charge, Luke wasn't feeling all that sure when his boy confidently announced they had arrived at their destination.

"You sure?" He felt silly questioning a kid, but he had no idea if they were at the right apartment or not, and he didn't even have his wife's cell phone number to call her and ask.

Charlie nodded and reached on tiptoes to push the buzzer.

Just when Luke was ready to call off the idea, Olivia's clear voice rang out through the intercom.

"Bolton residence, who is it?"

Luke swallowed. "Olivia?"

"Mom, it's me! Let us up!"

That solved the problem of explaining why they were there.

"Hey, honey, come on up."

Luke followed, starting to get used to the idea of being the one who did as he was told, rather than the other way around. Perhaps his son was destined to follow in his footsteps. The idea put a smile on his face as they walked up.

Charlie bounded on ahead and, breathless, jumped into the elevator. "You just push the button and it takes you to the right floor," he explained.

"Righto." Luke nodded.

Seconds later the doors swished open and they stepped

into an apartment like he'd never seen before. *Wow*. The guy clearly had plenty of money.

Jealously made Luke grimace, but he shrugged it away. Perhaps if he knew the man wasn't actually interested in Olivia he'd feel differently.

"Hi, sweetheart!" Ollie enveloped Charlie in her arms and kissed his head. "What are you two doing here?"

She directed that question at Luke, and he stuffed his hands deep into his pockets, feeling uncomfortable. He didn't like being in another man's house, especially when he wasn't exactly sure how to explain himself.

"We were at the park and Charlie decided he wanted to see you," Luke told her. "I hope we haven't interrupted."

Charlie hung on to his mom's leg, too preoccupied to chime in and tell her that they were here because Luke had told a strange woman at the park that's where they were heading.

"Nice place your boss has," he said.

Olivia smiled and turned back to the kitchen, Charlie trailing after her. "It's not exactly a bad place to work," she said over her shoulder. "Do you two want lunch?"

Charlie was already nodding, and Luke just smiled when she turned around to face them.

"How about you both sit down and I'll whip something up," she said.

Luke walked around the living room, his eyes picking up on all the things around him. Photos lining one side-piece, the odd painting, plus a few stacks of magazines and a couple of pricey-looking artifacts. Nothing over the top, but everything in the room looked expensive.

He stopped at the cluster of photographs and squinted, not liking what he saw. A handsome, dark-haired man was smiling back at him, his arm slung around a woman.

He was in most of the shots, and it didn't take a genius to work out that the man was the owner of the place.

"Is this your boss?" Luke asked.

Olivia hardly even looked up. "You mean the one with the pretty blonde? That's Ricardo with his sister."

Luke couldn't help the tight clench of his jaw. She obviously knew the photos intimately and he hated it. He could only hope that she was so familiar with them because she dusted around them regularly, not because she liked looking at her boss.

Jealousy wasn't an emotion Luke was familiar with, and he wasn't liking it at all.

"Lunch is ready."

He forced a smile and walked to the counter, trying to ignore the soft sway of his wife's hips, the way she smiled as their son ate his crusts, and the shine in her eye when she laughed. Olivia might be Luke's wife, but he had no right to be jealous of the people she knew, or who was in her life right now. But seeing her boss, acknowledging his jealousy toward him, was only making Luke want to fight all the more for what he'd lost.

Olivia was struggling not to smile as she finished her work. Charlie often came with her while she was here, but he usually played with his toys or pestered her about what he could do and when they'd be leaving. It was different having Luke here with him.

He'd taken Charlie out for a walk, then come back to wait for her. The two of them were hanging out on the sofa, Charlie tucked into the crook of Luke's arm, yabbering away. And now that she'd finished dinner for tonight and tomorrow, she was ready to go.

"Mommy, can we take Dad to the ice cream shop?"

Olivia laughed. It seemed that Charlie thought his dad was a playmate rather than a grown-up.

"Sure," she called out. "Just let me rinse this cloth out and we're out of here."

"Anything I can do to help?"

Olivia drew in a deep breath. Luke was watching her, his eyes trained on hers. Too close for her not to feel jittery. "Uh, no, I'm just about done."

He nodded. "Okay, I'll tidy up the cushions on the sofa and get Charlie's sweater on."

Now it was Olivia who was nodding. She didn't trust her voice. When Luke was at a distance, with Charlie, anywhere so that she was the one observing him rather than being up close and personal, she was fine. Close range turned her into a ball of knots.

She took one last look around, flicked the light switch and walked toward her son. "Let's go."

They stepped into the elevator and Olivia found it hard to breathe. Being with Luke like this, as if nothing was wrong, as if they'd always been this way, was making her uncomfortable. Because it felt as if they were living a temporary lie. With lies always came hurt, and she knew she had more of that coming, by the bucket load.

As they walked out onto the sidewalk, side by side with Charlie in the middle, Olivia couldn't help thinking how normal they must look to passersby. A mommy and daddy out for a nice afternoon with their child, without any hint of their dysfunctional reality.

"Swing me!" demanded Charlie.

That made Olivia smile. He always wanted to be swung, but she rarely had another adult with her to do it.

"Come on, then," she agreed.

Charlie held up both hands. She grasped one, then looked over at Luke. He appeared confused.

"We have to each hold one hand, then swing him forward as we walk," she explained.

Luke did as he was told, but Olivia could see from the look on his face that he had no idea what it was all about. She guessed he'd never had anyone swing him as a kid.

Charlie squealed with delight as he launched forward and it made Olivia happy to see him so excited. Having Luke home had been hard emotionally for her, but to Charlie it was like an ongoing party, a sleepover with a friend each day.

"I can see why he likes this."

Olivia grinned at Luke. "Let's do every second stride."

"One, two, three!" Luke was laughing so hard as Charlie swung that he could hardly count out aloud.

"Again, again!" Charlie squealed.

Olivia rolled her eyes at Luke. "One thing you realize with kids is they *always* want it again and again."

Her laughter died when she met Luke's gaze. His eyes were alive, dancing with pleasure as they continued to swing Charlie. She could feel the same flicker in her own—of hope—and for the first time since Luke had returned, she thought that maybe, just maybe, they actually did have a chance.

"Ice cream," announced Charlie. He dropped their hands and bounded on ahead.

Olivia fought the urge to look at Luke again before following her son, quickening her pace to keep up with him.

The sun had started to melt their ice cream into a sticky mess. Olivia ate the last of her cone and then went to Charlie's assistance. He had big globs of chocolate dripping down his chin, adorning his fingers and even the tip of his nose.

"You sure taught him how to eat an ice cream well."

Olivia grinned at Luke as she attacked Charlie with a wad of tissues. "Mmm-hmm."

They both laughed as Charlie ran in a circle to stay away from her, the last of his ice cream dripping on the ground.

"Charlie." Olivia used her firmest voice and tried not to smile.

His avoidance tactics continued.

"Charlie, *stop.*"

Luke's commanding voice rang out and the boy stopped dead in his tracks. Olivia rolled her eyes at Luke, but inside she was amazed. The little devil never listened to her when it came to things like this, but he was on his best behavior for his dad.

"Good boy," she said, wiping his face.

"Hey, Charlie?"

He looked up at his dad's voice.

"You need to listen to your mom, bud." Luke gave him a nod and a wink, as if letting him in on a secret. "She's pretty special and she's the only mom you've got."

Olivia shut her eyes for a heartbeat, still not sure how the hell they'd ended up here. How things were so normal and so weird all at the same time.

"Yeah?" asked Luke, his eyes on Charlie.

"Yeah," Charlie agreed before finishing the rest of his cone.

"Liv!"

Olivia turned at someone calling her name.

"Kelly! You're back from your vacation already?" She hugged her friend and bent to say hello to her little girl. "Hey, Bec, how are you, sweetheart?"

The girl twirled the edge of her skirt and looked away shyly, but Olivia knew this game. She gave her a quick kiss on the cheek and straightened again.

It took her only a second to realize she hadn't introduced her friend to Luke, who was looking uncomfortable, sitting on the bench alone. Charlie was showing off to Bec, just as he always did, goofing around and being silly.

"Uh, Kelly, this is Luke. Luke, Kelly." She gestured with her hand, suddenly confused. Should she go stand next to Luke or stay beside Kelly?

Luke smiled and stood. "Nice to meet you."

Her friend nodded and smiled, but Olivia could feel the tension and knew exactly what Kelly must be thinking. She'd made it clear what her thoughts were on husbands walking out, and it sure wasn't in Luke's favor. Even if Olivia *had* been honest with her about accepting some of the blame for the demise of her marriage.

"We've just had ice cream. Luke's been hanging out with Charlie at the park and..." She knew she was blabbing, but the tension in the air wasn't exactly helping her to stay relaxed. "What have you two been doing?"

Kelly was still looking at Luke, but the question seemed to snap her out of it. "The visit to my parents' place was pretty hectic, not much of a vacation." She reached out and touched Olivia's arm. "How have you been?" Her voice was lower, but Luke was standing less than two yards away.

"Fine, great. Anyway, we best get going," Olivia said.

Luke excused himself to follow Charlie, leaving her to deal with her burning hot cheeks alone. Talk about embarrassed!

She watched as he walked off, hands stuffed into his pockets, probably feeling like a complete outsider. And she hadn't done anything to make him feel more at ease.

"Daddy!" Charlie flung himself against his dad when he realized he was being followed, and Luke swung him up into the air and onto his shoulders.

Olivia watched, unable to look away.

It was things like that she felt sad about, or had felt sad about before, when she'd seen other kids with their dads. It wasn't that she didn't have a great time with her son, but seeing Luke play with him, tussle with him, made her cringe. Some things men were just better at than women. Like play fighting, Letting kids ride on their shoulders, pretend gunfights…all things she loved seeing fathers and sons do together.

"Liv, you're drooling. Snap out of it." Kelly laughed, but Olivia didn't miss the concern in her voice.

"Sorry, it's just…" What?

"You still love him." Her friend's voice was firm. No nonsense. "You want him back and he doesn't deserve it."

"Don't be ridiculous!" Even as she said it, another flood of heat rushed to her cheeks.

"Come on, Liv." Kelly put her arm around her shoulders and pulled her close. "You don't want to let him go. Be honest with yourself. It doesn't make you weak—it just makes you human."

Olivia wanted to pull away, but she knew her friend was right. They might have known each other only a couple of years, but two single moms covered a lot of history, and spent a lot of time talking. Olivia was wishing she hadn't been quite so honest with her friend now that Luke was home, though. All she knew was that he'd left Olivia and Charlie, and Kelly probably hated him for it. She hadn't known how things had been between them.

"You haven't given him the divorce papers, have you?" her friend asked, her voice soft and full of concern.

Olivia shook her head. "I tried but…no."

"It's your life, Liv, and I'll support you no matter what. I just don't want you to get hurt again."

"It's just…I…" Olivia searched for the right words.

"Seeing him with Charlie, having him back. It's tough." She fought the stinging tears that threatened to spill. "Tougher than I thought it would be, that's for sure. Just seeing him again has brought it all back, the good *and* the bad. And it wasn't all his fault, Kel. I have to take some ownership of that."

Kelly squeezed her around the waist and stepped back. "Just be careful, okay? Promise me that."

Olivia looked into her friend's eyes and saw the depth of her concern. She was lucky to have someone looking out for her, and she did appreciate her support. Her words of wisdom, too. Trouble was, unless Olivia walked away from Luke, or plain kicked him out, there was nothing she could do to be careful. She didn't want to get hurt, either, but it was hard. *Impossible*. She'd be hurt either way, regardless of how things worked out between them. All she had control over was making sure Charlie didn't get dragged into the middle of it all.

"You go catch up to him. Call me later. And be strong!"

Olivia dropped one hand to Bec, who had stood quietly at her mom's side while they chatted, and blew her a kiss before walking away.

"Thanks, Kelly. Love you," she called back as she followed her boys. Olivia could have all the strength in the world and not be able to fight off Luke Brown. He might have disappeared from her life these past couple of years, but seeing him again, being with him, had brought it all tumbling back.

Every time they were close, every time they touched, or laughed at something, it reminded her. She'd thought when he came back that she'd want to distance herself from him. That there'd be nothing left between them—no spark, no desire, no longing.

How wrong she'd been.

Because Luke was more than just the father of her child. He'd gotten under her skin again already, and she couldn't decide whether she wanted to get rid of him or hold on tight and never let him go.

Luke stood at the entrance to the kitchen, watching Olivia. He'd never stopped thinking about her, even when he'd tried his hardest to block her from his thoughts, but he'd never imagined he'd come back and feel like *this*. Like he'd do anything to turn back time, to change the way he'd left and the way things had soured between them.

He'd run when he should have stayed and faced their problems like a man, and for that he'd never forgive himself.

"You want me to help?" he asked, not sure what else to say to announce his presence, and not wanting to be caught staring at her.

"Everything's under control," she said, glancing up at him under her lashes before looking down again. "But sometimes it does feel like I spend all my life in the kitchen."

"Well, it smells great."

Olivia was stirring a pot of something on the stove, and he edged closer to take a look, *and to get closer to his wife*. After the junk he'd eaten for years, being back here was like eating at a gourmet restaurant each night, and he loved that Olivia was cooking for him.

"Actually, could you call Charlie to the table?" She looked up again, this time connecting with him instead of shying away.

He smiled, wanting her to feel at ease, to let her know that he was as uncertain about what was happening between them as she was. "Sure thing."

He went to the hallway. "Charlie, dinner's ready."

A burst of noise indicated Charlie had heard him. A door banged, followed by his son launching himself down the hall.

"Here," Charlie said.

"What is it?" Luke asked.

They boy frowned. "A picture."

Luke chuckled as he took it from him. Of course it was a picture.

He scanned the squiggly lines and tried to figure it out without asking for a clue.

"It's me, you and Mom."

Huh. He guessed it could be, if he squinted. Kind of.

"What's the big round thing over here?"

Charlie was already walking off, leaving Luke to trail behind, still looking at the drawing.

"It's a plane," Charlie told him.

"You like planes, huh?"

Charlie shook his head vigorously. "I hate planes. They take you away from us. That's why I put it there."

Luke felt an ice-cold press of dread. Wow. Talk about a kick in the guts. By a four-year-old.

"I'm not going to fly off and leave you again, Charlie. I'm not." He wished he could make his son realize how determined he was not to let him down again.

Charlie had settled himself at the table. Luke kept his voice low, not wanting Olivia to hear what they were talking about.

"I promise, bud. I'm not gonna leave you, okay?"

Charlie smiled but didn't look convinced. "I'm hungry."

"It's coming now," Olivia called out.

Luke stood back, fighting the urge to either walk from the room to find somewhere to be alone, or grab his kid hard and hold him tight, until he convinced him how much he cared. Because he'd done to his son what he'd hoped never to do. What he would regret for the rest of his life.

He'd given a little kid issues, and he had no excuse for it. He should have known better. But when Luke had finally come to his senses, he'd thought he'd come back in time. A four-year-old should be worrying about what toy to play with, his favorite television shows, and instead Charlie was worried about keeping his father here. About a parent not coming home again. Luke had never wanted a child of his to know what it was like to have a dad, then have him snatched away, but that's exactly what he'd done. Just because Luke hadn't died didn't mean his son had felt the loss any differently.

If he hadn't been sure before, he was now. It was time to break that cycle, to be a man and step up to his responsibilities. What worried him was the knowledge that if he hadn't almost died over there, he might never have realized what an idiot he'd been, and hightailed it back home.

"Dinner's ready."

Olivia stood at the table across from him. She had an apron tied around her middle, her hair pulled back off her face into a ponytail, and her cheeks were flushed from standing over the stove. Luke had everything to fight for, so why the hell had he been such an idiot?

He knew why. He'd met Olivia, thinking she was pretty and fun, and then it had turned into something more without him even realizing that fact. He had fallen for her hard, but he'd always planned to leave, and they'd never planned on having a baby. Hell, he'd never even thought about marriage until Olivia had taken the home pregnancy test. Then reality had come calling.

But the army had been his life, and when Charlie arrived Luke had faced the hardest decision he'd ever had to confront. And all he'd been able to think was that he should have kept walking, that first day he'd set eyes upon Olivia. If he'd kept walking, he would never have had to deal with being a dad, when he'd never wanted to be one. Or being married to a woman who deserved so much better.

"Luke?"

Olivia had sat down at the table next to Charlie. They were waiting for him. His perfect little family was watching him, wondering why he was standing still and staring at them like that.

He shook himself from his trance. "Sorry, I was a million miles away."

She started to dish food onto their plates, and Luke sat down. They'd been waiting for him a long time, his family. If he logically figured out what he had to do, it was to make them both—Olivia and Charlie—realize that he had been worth the wait.

Luke had to be honest, and make them understand just how hard his decision to stay away from home had been.

CHAPTER SIX

OLIVIA HADN'T BEEN able to think about anything other than
Luke since they'd seen Kelly. Now Charlie was tucked up
in bed, and that meant they had to talk about the tough
stuff. *Now*. Before she lost her nerve and ended up calling
it a night and heading for bed.

She doubted Luke wanted to talk about the past any
more than she did, but it was a conversation they had to
have, and as soon as he came back with their coffee, it
was time to start.

"Luke, I'm sorry about today."

He placed her mug in front of her and sat in the chair
opposite the sofa she was curled up on.

"It's no big deal. I like that you have a friend looking
out for you."

Olivia grinned. "More like a mama grizzly bear showing her teeth every time you looked at her."

Luke laughed, but their burst of humor was short-lived.
The expression on his face sobered as his eyes met hers.

"Do you think Charlie's coping? With having me
back?"

Olivia knew the answer to that. She thought Luke probably did, too. It wasn't as black-and-white as how he was
coping *now*, but rather was how he would cope *if*.

"He's doing fine, Luke. We just need to make sure he

does fine after." She wasn't going to mince words. She owed Luke the truth and he owed her the same. If they were ever going to consider how things could work for them, actually consider if they could ever build a future again, being honest was the best place to start.

The words hung between them, silenced their conversation. She stared into her coffee before looking back up. It wasn't time to falter; it was time to be real. And that meant dealing with the tough stuff.

"Luke, we're talking around things, talking around what happened, but we're never going to move forward unless..." She paused and watched as his fingers worked the fabric of a cushion. Then she took a deep breath. "I know things were bad between us, and I know that we're both to blame, but I still can't understand how you left. Do you have any idea what it did to me?"

He kept his eyes down. "Yeah."

No, he didn't, and she needed him to look at her. "How could you know? You were with your army family and I was alone. Bringing up a baby on my own, with no support, no help."

He was silent. When he looked up his features were almost haunted, if that was possible, showing his emotions like she'd never seen them before. But she was glad. He deserved to know, to *feel,* how painful his leaving had been for her. How hard it had been to care for Charlie, to deal with her husband leaving and a child, with no one to lighten the load. She wasn't saying it was all Luke's fault, but when he'd never returned...

"I suffered every day, too, Ollie. Just not in the same way." His voice was deep, husky, so low she had to listen hard to hear what he was saying.

It wasn't that she didn't believe him. For goodness' sake, he'd lived in a war zone for years! But what she'd felt was another kind of pain. The pain of a heart that had been shattered into a million tiny shards, like a smashed pane of glass. A heart she knew could never heal, but would remain wounded. A heart that had been given to him, that she had trusted him with, when she'd never thought she'd be able to let a man in.

But maybe that was the problem: she'd never truly believed that Luke had wanted to marry her, and part of her still didn't.

"It was hard for me, too, Ollie. It was so, so hard."

She wasn't enjoying this conversation one bit. Anger swept up her spine like an angry snake, curling around her shoulders and snapping at her throat, even though she wanted to be compassionate.

"I didn't think you were ever coming home, Luke. I never, ever thought I'd see you again." She fought her anger, her tears. "I had to grieve for you, never knowing, always waiting."

What had he thought when he'd left? That she was going to wait around forever until he decided he was man enough to come back? If he ever decided to come back…

His silence told her he thought otherwise. Had he always planned on coming home one day, or were there times when he'd thought about turning his back for good?

"I never intended on leaving him."

Olivia hated that Luke always referred to Charlie. The motherly side cherished that he loved his son, but the hurting, wanting woman in her wished he would say *her*. That he hadn't meant to leave *her,* that he'd thought about *her* every day.

"You were always there. In my mind." Luke looked up, his fingers thrumming impatiently against his jeans-clad thigh. "I never forgot what I'd left behind, Ollie. And while I know that might be hard for you to understand, I need you to believe me."

She wanted to believe him, but trusting Luke again, believing in his words, was going to take time. "You need to prove yourself to me, Luke. Words are meaningless without action."

He hung his head for a moment, then suddenly sat upright. As if someone had commanded him to, he braved her gaze, and met her eyes with a new intensity that almost made her falter. But there was one thing on her mind that she needed to say, to get off her chest now before she regretted it.

"I was faithful to you, Luke. I have always been faithful to you. I might have moved on with my life out of necessity, but I never forgot that I was married, and I need you to know that. No matter what I said or did before you left, I loved you."

A warmth filled Luke's brown eyes, a softness that showed itself in the slant of his shoulders as he leaned forward, in the way he stopped gripping his coffee cup as if he were trying to break it.

"Were you?" she asked, the words catching in her throat. The thought of Luke being with another woman, even kissing another woman, made her feel sick. A hot, clammy sweat broke out on her forehead. She could taste bile in her mouth. "Faithful?"

"I—"

"No." Olivia put up her hand to silence him, shuddering at the thought of his response. "You know what? Don't answer that. I don't want to know."

He smiled, a kind, relaxed smile that eased her fears. "I never forgot that we were married, either, Olivia. I promise."

That she hadn't been expecting. Her heart had been hammering, waiting for him to confess that he hadn't been so dedicated to the vows they'd made. But if he was telling her the truth, then maybe, just maybe, there was a flicker of possibility that they *could* work things out. Relief washed over her.

"It wasn't that I didn't move on, Luke. I did." She pushed through the pain of talking about all those months that she'd been on her own. "You were gone from me, as if the army had swallowed you up. I *had* to move on. But I couldn't move on that far, because I never really let go."

He moved from the chair to the sofa, sitting beside her. Olivia let him take her hand, watched as his fingers interlaced with hers.

"Ollie, I don't deserve your forgiveness, but I haven't exactly been honest with you about why staying in touch was so difficult for me."

She didn't get it. "What do you mean?" Excuses were not something she needed to hear.

Luke looked uncomfortable. He wasn't good at talking, never had been. He was a listener, and a darn good one, but she knew he'd be finding this difficult.

"When they called me up again, it was for a major promotion. I, uh…these past couple years I've been in Delta Force. An elite Special Forces operative."

The coin dropped. So he'd had a major reason to leave. He still could have explained to her, could have talked through his leaving, but hearing there was more to it than him just wanting to walk away took at least a little edge off her pain.

"It doesn't explain why I left like I did, but I need you to know that I was doing something that counted. I was so damn scared of wrecking things at home, and what did I end up doing? Turning my back for the sake of the army, and sacrificing you and Charlie."

"Delta Force?" she asked, still unable to believe that

she'd thought he was in standard service, while he was actually part of a Special Forces task force.

She remembered Luke talking about those guys. Always the most dedicated, secretive and tough men on tour, they often had to immerse themselves in a different way of life, travel constantly, and stay focused on the bigger picture. And from what she remembered, they were usually single. Had he been living under a different identity these past two years?

"It was restricted information, but I still should have found a way to tell you something." He paused, one hand raking so viciously at his hair she thought he might pull it out. "I'd been training for this my entire life, Ollie. My entire life. I never expected to be a dad, but I know now that our son should have been my priority. But they offered me the job and I jumped."

"Were you even in the Middle East?

Luke shook his head, a frown dragging his eyebrows downward.

"Afghanistan?" Tears stung her eyes but she pushed them away. She hadn't even known where he was! Her own *husband.*

"I had to immerse myself in a different culture. Grow a beard, learn the language. The whole nine yards." He kept hold of her hand even though she tried to pull away from him. "It doesn't excuse my actions, but I want you to know that what I did at least counted for something."

She didn't know what to say, felt like a fool for not even guessing that he'd been on some sort of confidential mission.

"It wasn't easy, Ollie. But it was what I'd been training for my whole life." He paused. "It's not an excuse, but I want to be honest with you, and telling you what I've been doing is part of that."

This was why their relationship had started to show cracks: because he thought she resented the army. But it wasn't that, couldn't be further from it. What she resented was that he thought his comrades were more his family than she was, *and that hurt*. Charlie was his real family. The fact that he'd promised to leave the army had been important to her, but him deciding to fight for their country again was not something she would ever have stopped him from doing. She'd faced a lifetime of lies before her tenth birthday—a lifetime of failed promises—so when Luke had made her a promise, the one person she'd *chosen* to trust in this world, she'd expected him not to let her down.

"Ollie?"

"I don't know what you want me to say, Luke."

He looked awkward, his eyes traveling from her hands to her eyes. When he reached for her other hand, she tried to ignore the pull of her body toward his. The way she so desperately wanted to feel him in her arms again, to remember what his touch was like, how he smelled, how masculine he was.

But she needed to stay strong.

"What I want is for you to understand," he said.

Olivia retrieved both her hands from his and tucked them around herself.

"You need to prove yourself to me before I'll understand, Luke. Whatever happened between us, whoever's fault it was, that's in the past. But if we're ever going to move forward, I need to believe what you're telling me."

His eyes locked on hers, but he didn't say anything. She met his gaze, determined to stay strong. She guessed he was telling her that he intended on doing just that, but she wasn't convinced. Because he could have told her more before he left, instead of waiting until now.

Delta Force. The words wouldn't stop repeating in her

mind, as if on a stuck cycle. How could he have been so far away, doing something so dangerous, without her knowing? Because the truth of it was that Luke could have died, and she would never have even known where he was. Or that he was *gone*.

CHAPTER SEVEN

TODAY HAD BEEN NICE. *More than nice.* It had almost felt normal. They'd dropped Charlie at preschool, done the grocery shopping together, just mundane things, but it had been good.

"Want to stop for something to eat?"

"Sure thing."

It was nice being the passenger in her own car and having someone drive her around for a change. And it was also nice not to be angry. Not to be seething inside and itching for a fight. It wasn't as if she'd forgiven Luke completely, but she was slowly opening up to the idea of listening to what he had to say, to giving him that chance to prove himself.

All Olivia had ever wanted was an explanation, a grown-up discussion about what he'd done and how it had hurt her and Charlie. The effect it had had on them. They'd made good headway yesterday, though the whole Delta Force announcement had thrown her a little. But still… She could see it from his point of view—not that she agreed, far from it. But if they were going to attempt a trial to see if they could ever be together again…she was going to have to *try.* And that meant she had to listen to him.

"Here okay?" he asked.

She looked out and saw the sign for Cup. Perfect. "Good choice," she said. Her stomach was starting to growl.

Luke pulled into the parking lot and turned off the engine. "How long do we have till Charlie's finished?"

"Another hour," she said.

They got out of the car and walked in. It was strange, being just the two of them. Since he'd been home almost all their time alone had been limited to the house. *And arguing.* It was as if Charlie was their buffer, ensuring they didn't argue too much, too loudly or too often.

This was like an awkward second date.

"Coffee?"

Olivia nodded. "Latte, please."

Luke ordered, then joined her at the table she'd chosen. He sat across from her, fingers thrumming gently on the tabletop.

"What's a normal day for you?" he asked.

Olivia looked up. "Is it weird transiting back to this kind of life?"

"Yeah."

She breathed a sigh of relief, needing to hear him say that. Because she *knew* he'd be finding it hard—missing his buddies, not sure how to fit back in at home.

"My days are pretty routine. I usually get Charlie up and ready, then it's either off to preschool or doing chores around home. Afternoons are most likely work for me, unless Charlie's at school, and then I do as much as I can."

Luke was watching her so intently she found it hard to look back. She'd never been so grateful to see a waitress when theirs arrived and placed coffee in front of them, because it gave her something to focus on other than the seriously masculine man sitting across from her. It didn't seem to matter what the time of day or what he was wearing, she couldn't stop the insistent thud of attraction that continually pushed through her body. A yearning she couldn't control, a desperation to know what it would be like to be back in his arms again, even though she resented thinking like that at all.

"Two forks. Enjoy."

Olivia murmured a thank-you, but she was focused on Luke and the plate in front of her.

"What's this?"

Clearly she knew what it was, but...

"You don't like lemon meringue pie anymore?"

She did. Oh, did she ever. But how had he remembered something like that?

Luke leaned over the table and handed her one of the forks. "There are things I'll never forget about you, Ollie. Pie is only one of them."

She reached for the fork and took a mouthful, savoring the sweet yet tart flavor. It had always been her favorite dessert, her weakness. And somehow, despite everything that had happened between them, all the time that had passed, Luke hadn't forgotten.

He winked at her, that delicious slow wink that never failed to make her body turn to liquid. "We used to be good, you and me. Before life got all complicated on us."

It was times like this she could almost pretend he'd never left.

Luke watched her from across the table. He couldn't have dragged his eyes from her even if he'd wanted to.

"You first," he said, sliding the plate her way.

Olivia looked at him, before shrugging and taking another mouthful.

"Good?"

She giggled and put her hand in front of her mouth. "Definitely worth getting fat for."

She took another few mouthfuls before pushing it back toward him. "Thank you."

Luke looked up from the pie. "For what?"

She shrugged her shoulders before sitting back in the chair, as if she wasn't sure what she wanted to tell him. Or maybe she was, but didn't know how to say it.

"For this," she said, her voice low. "For remembering."

As if he would ever forget about her. "When we married, we were so young," he said, hoping it came out the right way. "After what I've seen, the things I've been witness to, I don't want to argue, Ollie. I just want to give us a real chance." Luke paused. "I had a lot of time to think when I was away, time to try to figure out where we went wrong, and you know what?"

Olivia hadn't taken her eyes from him.

"I think things might have been different if we'd taken it slow. If we hadn't rushed headfirst into marriage and a baby, even though we didn't really have any control over that." He smiled at her, wishing they could go back in time. "But I'd like to think we could start over again and go slow. Or at least consider it."

She looked up before reaching for the fork resting on the side of the plate, and diverting her gaze. "I'd like that," she said, her hand hovering midair as she met his gaze again. "I just hope we're not already past the point of no return."

Luke didn't look away until she did. He hoped she was wrong about that.

"So tell me more about Charlie's preschool," he asked.

Olivia looked relieved that he'd changed the subject. "If we start talking about how brilliant that kid is at preschool we could be here all day."

Funny, but Luke didn't mind the sound of that. Not one bit.

* * *

Olivia smiled across the room at him and Luke grinned straight back. Every smile, every touch, every gesture made him feel as if he was getting somewhere. That having to work so hard was worth every scrap of effort.

When he'd been in foster care, times had never been easy. He'd learned to appreciate every minor victory, every day that didn't result in a beating or a bad word. Every day that didn't make him cry for the father he'd lost. And that was how he was approaching being part of his family again. Every day that went by without him messing up was a good one. A day he could be proud of. And one that made his regret that he'd ever left them run even deeper.

The one thing that was tough was not being particularly good at what he was trying to do. When he joined the army, he'd trained harder than any of the other recruits, he'd worked harder to ascend the ranks and he'd learned with rapid speed when he'd been accepted into Delta Force. But there was no course, no training, no *anything* to practice when it came to being a dad. Being a great father meant learning through mistakes, and that was not something that came naturally to Luke. He liked rules, orders, strategies—but he was darned if he was going to give up this time without doing his best. Even if there wasn't a rule book for him to follow.

Olivia's voice made him look up. She'd walked back into the room.

"Would you mind taking care of Charlie tomorrow afternoon, Luke?"

No, he didn't mind at all. "Sure."

Olivia gave him a smile. He wished he knew if it was a thanks-for-helping-out kind of smile, or something more.

She picked up some of Charlie's clothes and started to fold them. "I need to help Ricardo prepare for a party, but it shouldn't take long. It just means I'll be back later than usual."

Ricardo. Luke hated every syllable, every letter, of that man's name. He knew it was stupid, but there was something he didn't like about the guy, or the way Olivia spoke about him.

"Luke?"

He tried not to show the jealousy throbbing at his temple.

"Sure. Fine. We'll just hang out here."

She smiled again, and this time he knew it wasn't the smile he'd been hoping for.

"Charlie, did you tell your dad that it's your birthday soon?"

Luke watched his son, determined not to show how rattled he was, but inside his stomach was twisting like a Rubik's cube. Was she just saying that to see if he remembered? He knew the date, had never forgotten it, but he obviously had a long way to go before he could convince *her* of that.

"I'm gonna be four!" Charlie enthusiastically flicked the spaghetti he was eating for emphasis. "One, two, three, four!"

"And what do you want for your birthday, big guy?" His kid's excitement was contagious.

"Soldier toys."

Luke smiled, but reined it back when he saw how concerned Olivia looked.

"What else, honey?" she asked him.

Luke looked at Charlie, waiting for him to answer his mom's question.

"Guns!"

Luke cleared his throat. It wasn't that he didn't love that his boy liked soldiers and guns, because he'd always been the same, but he knew what a raw nerve it had probably just hit in his wife. Given the fact she looked as if she'd just sucked a lemon.

"Charlie, what about the lovely toys you wanted last week? The books?" Olivia persisted.

"I wanna be like Daddy. Bang, bang!"

Luke stepped up and removed the fork from his hand.

"Guns are serious, bud. You don't point them at your mom, and you don't use your fork like that."

Charlie stared back up at him, tears in his eyes. *Oh, sheesh.* Luke had tried to do the right thing and the kid was going to start bawling. Luke bent so he could look him in the eye.

"Don't cry, Charlie. We just need some rules, and I don't want you to upset your mom."

Charlie started wailing, fled the chair and flew into Olivia's arms, his little body heaving with sobs. Luke felt like an idiot. A mean, unloving idiot. Had he been too serious, too tough on his son? Wasn't he meant to be firm at times?

"Ollie, I'm sorry, I was just trying to say the right thing."

She shook her head, her lips on Charlie's blond hair. "He's just not used to you telling him off," she said, giving Luke what he guessed was a reassuring nod. "You've been his friend, and now he's seeing you as a parent."

Luke went to answer, then snapped his jaw shut as she carried their son to his room. Luke definitely needed to find that elusive manual on parenting. Maybe then he'd stop making a fool of himself at the worst of times....

Real fathers laid down ground rules, took charge, but he guessed that was the problem. Most dads did so since childbirth, whereas Charlie was used to being with his mom. Used to his mom's rules, his mom's love, his mom full stop.

Luke picked up his beer and took a good swig, until he realized Olivia had reappeared. He put it down on the side table and sat back in the chair.

"He must have been exhausted. Fell asleep in my arms and now he's tucked up in bed."

Luke nodded. She was trying hard, he could tell that. But so was he, only he wasn't succeeding in his mission.

"You know when we met, how I told you a little about my past but never wanted to talk about what had happened in foster care?"

Olivia lowered herself slowly into her chair, as if she was afraid that if she moved too fast he'd change his mind and stop talking. "I remember, Luke. You told me that you'd buried that part of your past and had no intention of ever digging it back up."

He shut his eyes and let his shoulders fall, leaning deeper into the chair. Talking about his past was never going to be easy, but right now, it was the only way he could think to open up to Olivia. To make her understand.

"Maybe if I'd dug it up, back when you'd asked me about it, we wouldn't be here now."

She looked sad, her head on an angle as she stared at him. As if she couldn't believe what he was saying. "You mean we never would have gotten married?"

"No, Ollie. I mean that maybe we could have avoided all the hard stuff. That it wouldn't be like *this*. That you could have understood what I meant when I told you I didn't want to be a dad."

She tucked her feet up and wrapped her arms around her legs, knees drawn up tight to her chin. He knew he'd hurt her when he'd told her that, but back then he hadn't known how to express his fears, what he was so desperately afraid of.

"I know what it's like to remember a dad and know that he'll never come back," Luke said in a low voice. "To grow up with no one and wish that things could have been different, wish that you could turn back time. I can still remember flashes of what they were like, both of my parents, but then sometimes I wonder if I imagined it just to have something to hold on to."

Olivia had tears in her eyes now, threatening to spill down her cheeks. "I don't want that for Charlie, Luke. I don't want to see him wait for his dad his whole life."

Luke shook his head, steeled his jaw and tried to fight the emotion ripping through his own body. But he couldn't. He fell forward, on his knees, reaching for Ollie's hands and holding tight once he had them.

"Ollie, you need to believe me when I say I don't want to repeat that pattern. *Please.* And my leaving, that was me trying *not* to repeat it, trying to stop Charlie from knowing me and then losing me."

She let go of his hands and placed hers on his face instead, palms to his cheeks. "I'm trying, but it's not easy for me to understand."

Fear had gnawed him at every turn, haunted him when he was away at war. That he had no one. That he'd never had anyone. Yet here he was, with a woman who had once loved him and a son who was desperate to love him, and he'd already messed it up. He might have grown up alone, but he had the chance to be someone here, to be connected to people who loved him, and it was time he swallowed his fears and tried to confront them. His own fears, his not wanting to hurt his son like he'd been hurt, had only re-created his experience as a boy.

But it was now or never.

"Ollie," he whispered, turning his cheek into her hand.

This time when he looked up, she was biting down on her bottom lip, eyes holding his. He took his chance.

Luke pushed himself higher, still on his knees, and touched both of *his* palms to her cheeks. Took strength from the openness of her gaze as he slowly brought his lips to hers. Grazed his mouth softly against hers, paused, then deepened their kiss. Wanting to tell her so many things, but trying to show her instead. Because he'd opened up as much as he was capable tonight, and now he needed to know she at least wanted him as much as he still wanted her. Even if she wasn't ready to say so yet, he needed a hint.

"Luke," she murmured, her hand sliding up between them, as if she wanted to stop him but wasn't ready to just yet.

He pulled back slowly, not wanting to push her, wanting her in his arms, against his body.

Because at least now he knew that he had a chance. He had to believe that she wouldn't have kissed him back like that if there wasn't still *something* between them. Wouldn't have pushed herself against him if she hadn't wanted him, too.

"Good night," he whispered, trailing his fingers down her face and across her shoulders as he stood.

"You're going to bed?" He could hear the confusion in her voice. "Now?"

"Yeah." He chuckled as he took a step backward. "Because if I stay right here any longer, I don't know if I'll be able to stop myself."

Olivia flushed but didn't tell him to stay, so he gave her one last smile and headed for the spare room.

She was his wife, and he loved her. Now he only had to hope that she was falling back in love with him, too.

CHAPTER EIGHT

LUKE HAD NEVER seen so many toys. Big stuffed animals, robots, Lego—every shelf was filled with an endless array of kids' entertainment. To his credit, Charlie was behaving well, but some of the other children around them were starting to get on Luke's nerves.

Especially because of what he'd witnessed these past couple of years. The children he'd seen beyond excited over a piece of fruit, a loaf of bread, *anything* that meant they could quell their hunger pangs. Children who had no idea what a childhood really was, not by American standards, anyway, yet managed to smile at a friendly stranger. Managed to overcome their difficulties. And now he was surrounded by children with full bellies, begging their parents for the next latest and greatest toy as if their lives depended upon it.

"Luke, what do you think?"

Olivia and Charlie were inspecting something nearby. He walked over. They were looking at a display of trains.

"Dad, this is Thomas."

Charlie's face was alive with happiness and Luke felt like the Grinch for not being more enthusiastic. He found it hard to make distinctions between life here and life at war sometimes, but it was something he was going to have to get his head around. He had a great kid who hadn't been spoiled, and it was his *birthday.* Charlie deserved some great gifts.

"Dad?"

Charlie tugged on his jeans and Luke gave him his full attention. "It *is* Thomas." He bent down. "He's pretty cool."

"Don't you already have Thomas?" Olivia asked, taking the engine from his hands and putting it back. "It would be silly to have two of the same. How about some of his friends here?"

Luke grinned as he watched his son's attention divert to the other train.

"Percy!"

"Well done," Luke told her, edging closer so he could speak to her without Charlie hearing.

Olivia grinned, her entire face alight. He loved when she did that. It made him feel as if there was still something special between them, something drawing them together rather than pushing them apart.

"I've already bought Percy and another train called Diesel," she whispered, bringing her head close to his. "Now we'll take him past the DVDs, and if you stay put I'll get the new *Cars* one and a couple of books."

"Roger that," Luke whispered back, enjoying the feel of having Ollie near. What he would do to be able to pull her against him and just hold her. Smell her perfume, feel the warmth of her, and go back a few years, to start over. To leave on different terms, to tell her he loved her.

"Ollie…"

She fixed her eyes on his, the happy conspiracy of birthday shopping still lighting her face as he bent closer.

"Mommy! Mommy, look!"

Olivia gave Luke an apologetic smile, her pink lips far

too close to his for comfort, before turning her full attention back to Charlie.

I'm sorry. I love you. The words Luke wanted to say hung over him, the need to tell her even greater than his need to kiss her and pull her body against his. *I should never have let you go.*

Their bags were full to the brim with balloon packets, streamers, wrapping paper and presents for Charlie. Lots of little extra ones to make the big day fun. With Luke home, she wanted to make this birthday one he'd never forget.

Luke walked ahead with Charlie, and she trailed behind with the bag of gifts for him, cleverly concealed. She'd given Luke the party bags and Charlie hadn't suspected a thing.

She tried not to laugh as she watched them—Luke doing all the listening and Charlie asking all the questions and talking nonstop. It was one of the things she'd loved about Luke when they'd met, his ability to listen so well. Only trouble was at the time she hadn't realized how badly *she'd* needed to listen. That instead of lying awake worrying, taking on all their problems as her own and thinking Luke didn't want the life he was living with her, she should have been asking him. Making him talk. Being the listener he needed.

Luke had once listened to her for hours, always smiling, touching her as if he was happy just to watch and lend an ear. Back then, in the early whirlwind of falling in love, she'd hardly noticed that she knew so little about him, when he knew so much about her. Then she'd started to realize that Luke had deeper issues than even she did. And she'd wished she'd asked him more, pushed him harder to open up. Because if she had, maybe he wouldn't have thought that walking away was the right thing to do.

Olivia snapped out of her daydream and noticed them both leaning on the car. Luke's tall frame was propped against the vehicle, long legs stretched out in front of him. Charlie was doing his best to mimic his dad, and struggling. She tried not to laugh.

"How are my boys?" she called, walking faster to catch up to them.

"We're great." Luke's lazy smile made her heart skip. She hadn't seen *that* smile since he'd returned.

"Good."

She dug around in her bag for the keys and unlocked the car, but Luke grabbed her hand and swung her toward him before she could open it.

"Hey," he said, grinning as he held her tight.

She went to open her mouth, to say something back, when he planted a quick, cheeky kiss on her lips instead. His mouth hovered over hers, laughter in his eyes, before he pulled back.

Olivia touched her fingers to her lips—lips that were buzzing from the unexpected burst of affection from her husband.

"I love you," he whispered in her ear, before opening the door and holding it for her.

Olivia stood still, unable to move for a moment, before forcing her feet to comply.

I love you, too, she thought. But right now, she couldn't bring herself to acknowledge what he'd said, and tell him the same.

Olivia rested her elbows on the kitchen counter as she bent to inhale the sweet scent of the cake she'd just baked. It sat on a wire stand, cooling so she could ice it. The smell of it brought back memories of her childhood, when her mother would be in the kitchen and she'd be at the table watching her. They might not have had a lot of money, but her mom had sure known how to bake up a storm.

The only thing that hadn't been idyllic about that scene had been wondering when her dad was going to arrive home, or *if.* And if he did, whether or not she'd be told to scurry to her bedroom and close the door, so she didn't have to hear them arguing.

A shudder crawled up her spine and she closed her eyes. Once he'd gone, once her mother had finally kicked him out, life had become happier, more pleasant. There were no nights wondering why her father hadn't come home, no worries about him raising his voice in drunken anger while she shivered with fear beneath the sheets. But she had seen how it slowly ate away at her mom, and beneath their happiness together, the lovely life they had was tainted by her dad. Even once he was gone.

If only her mom was still alive. Here with her so they could talk.

"Penny for them?"

Olivia's eyes opened with a snap. She jumped to attention, elbows smashing hard against the counter.

"Luke! What are you doing up?"

He grinned at her. "Heard you crashing around in here and thought I'd help."

She could see the smile in his eyes. She hadn't been making a noise, and he knew it.

"Okay," he admitted, walking toward her. "I couldn't sleep and I knew you were in here."

She moved away from him, back toward the sink as he walked closer. She felt distinctly like an animal being watched, stalked by a lion. Only this predator was more scary than a lion. He didn't want to eat her—he wanted her heart.

"Want a glass of milk?"

"Yes, ma'am."

She couldn't help it; Olivia cracked a smile and tried her hardest not to laugh. That old-fashioned charm had always made her flutter inside. *The soldier has manners.* That's what she'd thought when she'd first met him, one of the first things she'd noticed about him, aside from how great he'd looked in a pair of too-long denim shorts and a T-shirt.

Olivia poured two glasses of milk and then turned back around. Luke was closer than she'd realized. He reached out and took one of the glasses from her. When he didn't move, she stepped out and maneuvered around him, desperate to keep that sense of distance between them.

"You okay?"

She nodded. What else could she do? Aside from tell him that her heart was beating way too fast and she wanted him so badly. Wanted his arms around her, his mouth on hers, and to stop thinking about what had happened and just let him love her.

"Just, uh, thinking about the party tomorrow," she said, trying to keep her eyes diverted from him. Especially from his low-slung pajama pants and bare chest.

Stop looking at his chest. Ignore the bare skin.

Luke drained his glass of milk and wiped his mouth.

"I feel like a kid who's had a nightmare," he teased. "Next time I might need it warmed."

She knew the truth behind those words, though. There had never been anyone to fill a glass of milk for Luke when he was a kid. He'd been a fighter, had to be, just to make it through to adulthood.

They stood there in silence. Luke tall like a statue in the

middle of the kitchen, her tucked around by the counter. She sipped at her milk—not something she would ordinarily drink, but perfect for now. If she'd poured a coffee she would be awake all night, if not bouncing off the walls.

"Luke, how are we doing?" She'd been rolling that question around in her mind all night. The cake had been baked on autopilot; she was lost to her thoughts and hoped she'd remembered all the ingredients. Hadn't put in salt instead of sugar, she'd been so absentminded.

Her question had him thinking. That slightly humorous, confident twinkle in his eyes had faded. Fast. Now he looked serious.

"I don't know, Ollie," he replied, his voice gravelly.

She toyed with the glass, her fingers gliding across the smooth surface. She pushed her shoulders up and then down in a gentle shrug. That was the problem. She didn't know, either.

"It's hard, being back." He nodded as he spoke. "If I'm honest about it, I'm liking it, but it's still hard."

That wasn't the answer she'd hoped for. It was *hard?* As in she was hard, being here was hard, what?

"Do you not want to be here?"

He closed his eyes for a second, inhaled deeply and then shook his head, almost sadly.

"It's hard being a civilian again, Ollie. It's not that I don't want to try, but it's just a big change. It's different, that's all, but I don't mean in a bad way."

Relief fluttered in her throat, like a leaf in the breeze.

He put his glass in the sink and stood, his back to her. Talking wasn't his thing, so she knew he'd be finding this difficult. But if he wanted a chance, a real chance like he'd asked for, he was going to have to learn how to talk. They couldn't be a team, stay married, unless they put all their cards on the table. And that meant that she had to become a listener.

"Tell me, Luke," she said.

"War is a completely different way of life," he told her, his voice a low rumble. "It *was* my life, and what I became used to doing, what I did every day and who I was surrounded with, so I'd be lying if I said that wasn't hard to leave behind."

He turned to face her, his eyes intense, searching hers. She stayed silent, stunned that he was finally talking about what he'd been doing, what the army meant to him. And she was craving every word of it.

"War becomes the real world. And where I was, that meant me being in charge. I made decisions. I wasn't questioned, because I made sure I made the right calls, and I knew how to be the best damn Special Forces soldier I could be. I stayed alive because I was good at what I did, and now back here I'm a no one." He sighed. "I'm back to being the guy who grew up with nothing and no one to give a damn about him, and worrying that I'm making mistakes every step of the way."

Olivia fought the desperate wish to shut her eyes and block out what Luke was saying. But she couldn't. Because she was the one who'd told him to be honest, told him about the importance of opening up to her, and now she had to deal with the reality of his words.

"Luke, you're not a *no one* here. You're a dad, and right now you're still my husband." She blew out a breath. Just admitting that made her realize how wrong she'd been in trying to fire the divorce papers at him when he'd first arrived back. "You don't ever have to be alone and unloved again. The difference now is that you have a choice."

He smiled, but she could tell there was still so much left unsaid, so much he needed to tell her before he could properly move on. Before they could start to move forward and build on what they'd once had.

"All I know is how to be a great soldier, Ollie, because I've worked at it for years. Here, I don't know how to do the right thing, how to be the dad Charlie needs me to be." Luke looked tortured, crestfallen. She had never, ever seen him like this—almost on the verge of tears. "All I want is a dad to show me the ropes, to give me a role model. Show me how to do what I need to do for Charlie. Tell me what an idiot I was for leaving, and thinking in some warped way that I was doing the right thing."

"You don't need a role model to do that, Luke," she said, trying hard not to cry herself. "You just need to be here, to *try,* to not be so hard on yourself." She crossed the room and stood before him, trying to ignore how scared she was. How much she was opening up and how easy it would be for Luke to hurt her if he walked away. "If I hadn't thought you'd be a great dad," she said, taking one of his hands and pressing it to her heart, "if I hadn't known it *right here,* I never would have had Charlie."

"You mean you thought about not having him?" he asked, eyes locked on hers.

"No." Olivia slowly shook her head, still staring at him. "I didn't have to think about it, because I knew the kind of person you were. That's why it hurt me so bad when you walked away. When you made my deepest fear a reality."

Luke's eyes were filled with tears now, and she could tell from the vein bulging across his forehead and the clamp of his jaw that he was struggling to compose himself.

"Charlie doesn't know any other dad, he only knows *you,* and he only wants you. We all make mistakes. It's what parenting is all about. But you just need to be *you,*

Luke. That's all you need to do to have a real second chance."

They watched one another, both standing dead still, so close that she could feel his breath on her face when he exhaled.

"What about being a husband, Ollie?" His voice was so deep now she almost looked away, his gaze so intense it scared her. "How do I go about being a better one of those?"

She didn't have an answer for that. There was no magic model, no criteria that she could list for him to fulfil. What she wanted was for him to figure it out, to prove to her that she could trust him, because right now she wanted to. She wanted to let him in and trust him more than she'd ever wanted to before.

"I don't know, Luke." It was the truth. "I don't know, but I do know that I want us both to figure it out."

The expression on his face hardly changed, but the difference in his body was impossible not to notice. Luke spun on the spot, his entire frame tense and rigid as he walked away.

And then he turned, fast. And this time his expression was dark, the look in his eyes terrifying and exhilarating all in the same second.

Luke moved with stealth toward her, his long strides eating up the space between them before she could even register what he was doing. He had never been one for words, never pretended that he liked flowery, lengthy discussions or over-the-top flattery. But what he did have on his side was a power and presence that could rival any man's. And with God as her witness, he was the most attractive, strong, addictive man she'd ever encountered.

Olivia's heart felt as if it had slid up into her throat, forcing her breath out in shallow bursts. He was virtually towering over her, his big frame dwarfing her, overpowering but not crowding her.

"How do I be a good husband, Ollie? Tell me how," he demanded.

If only she could. There was nothing in the world she wanted more than for Luke to be the husband she'd hoped for, but it was hard to forget the past. Trust was everything to her, and no matter how her body tried to disagree, she had to be careful, protect herself. Even if she did want him so badly she was almost slithering to the floor into a pool of liquid.

"How, Ollie?" he asked again. He was so close that she could feel each word as he punched it out, his mouth within dangerous proximity to hers. "Tell me *how*." His voice was deep, raspy, dangerous.

Luke stopped asking questions and reached for her chin instead, his thumb forcing her to meet his stare. There, she saw the pain in his eyes—the desperation mixed with need, much like what she felt inside.

She couldn't answer him. Her eyes were locked on his as if she was transfixed, her mouth clamped shut as if she was scared of opening it. Every hair, every pore of her body was on high alert.

"Just tell me how." His voice was barely a whisper now, cracked with emotion, and the tightness in her throat forced her to realize she was choking up, too.

"Luke…"

He didn't wait to hear her excuse, but kept his thumb under her chin and somehow shuffled his body even tighter against hers. She was stuck between the edge of the counter and a huge male frame, six foot four inches of lean muscle and determination. She swallowed a lick of excitement. Most of her wanted to run, but the part of her she couldn't defy was telling her to stay. To enjoy.

He brought his lips down to hers painstakingly slowly, until he was only a breath away. *Then he closed the remaining distance fast.* Kissed her so hard her fingers leaped to take hold of his arms, which snaked around her to keep her locked against his body.

Olivia consumed his kiss like an alcoholic searching for a sip of tequila, drowning in it like a junky floating in a drug-induced haze. It was as if she'd been sober for two long years, and she was finally fueling her addiction.

But her addiction wasn't for a substance, it was for a man who'd sent her crazy from the moment she'd first set eyes upon him. From their very first kiss. Their very first date. The very first night she'd spent in his arms.

His lips moved more desperately against hers, and Olivia didn't fight his embrace or his kisses. Luke scooped her up and placed her on the countertop, and she wrapped her legs right around his waist, forcing their bodies even closer.

"Mommy!"

Luke jumped a step back as a scream from down the hall pierced the silence around them.

Olivia blinked twice, still lost in the moment. Her hand fluttered to his mouth, still so close to hers.

"Mommy!"

"I'll go to him." Luke's voice was calm, deep.

She couldn't move. Olivia looked at Luke, at the flush of his cheeks, the ruffled mess of his hair. What had just happened? How had she let things get so out of control?

"Ollie?"

She snapped out of it. "Aah, he has nightmares. Are you sure…?"

"I'll go." Luke stepped closer to her again and kissed her cheek, his lips warm as they touched her skin.

Ollie watched him walk down the hall, then glanced at the bowl of unused icing.

So much for staying up late to finish the cake.

Instead, she'd let herself be seduced by her husband. And she'd more than enjoyed it.

She'd loved it.

CHAPTER NINE

OLIVIA FELT AS if she'd blown all the air out of her lungs. Balloons filled the room, a burst of colors that enlivened the white walls. She was trying to fill her mind with the party, with thoughts of the little boys who would be arriving soon, but she couldn't.

While Luke had been away, she'd thought about him a lot. When she was hating him, grieving for him, wishing for him—at every stage. But nothing beat the way she was thinking about him now. The way he moved, straight-backed and confident, like the soldier he was. The coil of his biceps when he reached for something, the breadth of his shoulders when he stood before her. Everything about him was making her think, making her *want,* and it was starting to drive her crazy.

A soft thud made her look up. Speak of the devil. She spotted him from the corner of her eye, saw him move through the kitchen and tried not to watch him. *It was an impossible task.*

Luke looked up. Heat made her cheeks burn as their eyes met—like a flame ignited with the strength of hell's fury. Olivia tried to look away, to break the stare, but she couldn't. Wouldn't. And neither did Luke.

"Hey." His voice was a low rumble.

Olivia swallowed. "Hi."

She tried to go back to blowing the balloons, but was out of breath. She'd blown up twenty-odd balloons in a row, but one word to Luke and she was suddenly incapable.

"The streamers are flying at the gate and the sign's up on the porch," he told her.

"Huh." Where were the witty words when she needed them? "Thanks."

"You okay?" Luke walked toward her. "Need a hand?"

She absorbed the snug fit of his white T-shirt, the tan of his bare feet, even the slight length of his hair. Mussed as if he'd just rolled out of bed.

Olivia gulped and passed him the balloon. He took it from her with a smile and pressed his lips to the opening. His steady breaths reminded her of his role as a soldier. Was he so kind, so thoughtful, so *steady* in the field?

She shook her head and pushed the thoughts away. When had she gone from thinking about him leaving them to describing him as thoughtful? The man had left them, *alone,* until he'd swept back into their lives last week. She needed to remember that and not get carried away with things like kissing in the kitchen the night before or...

"You sure you're okay?"

Luke's voice pulled her from her thoughts. "Yeah, I'm fine. Just a lot on my mind."

He gave one final blow, then tied the end in a knot. "All done now?" he asked.

"All done."

They stood looking at one another. Ollie kept trying to think about why they couldn't be together, why she could never trust him again. But he was making it hard. Her eyes trailed over his face. He just stared at her, the iron clamp of his jaw softening as he gazed back.

When Olivia looked away at last, she felt like a deer just

rescued from the glare of lights in the dark. She couldn't trust herself around him. The pull was too great and it was slowly, surely, breaking all her defenses. He was making her feel as if there was no way out, no way back, except into his arms. And she was wanting it more and more.

"Mommy!"

That did it. Saved by the kid again. Olivia stepped aside and moved in the direction of Charlie's voice.

"Ollie." Luke touched her arm, gripped her wrist and stopped her from moving. She looked up, a shiver catching in her back.

She thought he was going to kiss her, say something important, *anything*. But he just watched her, his gaze digging deep into her heart.

The moment passed. He let go. And Olivia walked toward her son's room. She could feel Luke still standing behind her. Not moving. Immobile, like a statue.

As she walked, she'd never felt more alone. Because this time she'd *wanted* him to do something, to kiss her again, to pull her into his arms, or to simply take her hand and walk with her down the hall.

But he'd done nothing.

Just like how he'd left her. Alone, when she'd been so desperate for his touch, desperate to tell him she was sorry and that she didn't want to fight with him anymore. And just like before, it was as if a wound had opened within her, raw and painful. Because Luke was the first person she'd ever truly trusted, and she wanted so badly to go back to that place again. Where she could trust him with all her heart and not be worrying about when he was going to leave, or that he was staying with her only out of duty. *Again.*

"Mommy!"

"I'm coming, honey," she called back. In one more step she was in his bedroom.

"Look!"

She looked down and couldn't help but smile. Luke had given him a gun for his birthday, but not the big, black, glossy one she had dreaded. It was carved from timber, a beautifully crafted toy that Charlie had hold of as if he'd never let go.

"Daddy made it himself. Can I show my friends?"

She nodded. "Sure thing."

Olivia sensed more than heard Luke behind them. She didn't know if she could even turn to acknowledge him. Every little thing that happened, every action that made them more like a family, terrified her. She had thought he'd make more mistakes, that it would be easier to blame him and push him away. But everything he did right now only seemed to make her want him more.

She kept her shoulders straight, determined to remain confident no matter how she felt. And sure enough, when she turned, those eyes were waiting for her, and she needed every ounce of her strength not to step into his arms. Those smiling, soft, concerned eyes that had been entrenched in her heart since the day she'd met him were focused on her. As if he could see straight through her and into every emotion pummelling her body.

"We all ready for the party?" he asked.

Ollie nodded. As ready as she'd ever be to introduce her husband to the friends she'd made in his absence.

"Will they be here soon?"

Charlie broke their spell. His little voice pulled their gazes from one another, reminding them that they weren't alone in the room.

"Let's get out there, kiddo," she said. "They'll all be here before you know it."

Luke shifted his weight from the doorjamb and she watched him move away. A ball of worry stuck in her throat. This was harder than she'd expected. A whole lot harder and then some.

The squeals of children echoed around the room and Luke's head started to pound. He wasn't used to this. The noise level was too much, too loud, too happy. He'd never heard anything like it. In war zones there was often noise, either hardly a sound or the reverberating of bullets like a curtain of terror. But even war was nothing like this.

Luke looked over at Ollie. Just the sight of her dulled the thumping in his head, the strain in his neck.

She was talking to a friend, a mother of one of the children. Her head was tilted slightly as she listened, mouth parted as she laughed, and Luke couldn't look away.

All his life he'd felt a hollow void within him at not knowing his family, at not having parents, at missing out on the childhood he could have had, had they been alive. There were plenty of other children at his school, in his life, who'd easily had it as rough as he had, so he'd never realized quite how much he'd missed. How much of the fun and joy he'd been deprived of as a child. Fun and happiness that his son was so lucky to be experiencing.

"Dad!"

Luke looked down to find Charlie tugging the leg of his jeans.

"Can you show them the soldier's wave?"

Luke guessed these kids didn't have soldiers for dads, but the last thing he'd wanted was to draw attention to himself. "They don't want to see, buddy," he told him.

Luke caught Olivia's gaze. She was watching him from across the room. So were some of the other moms.

He looked down at Charlie, who was pouting, his lips

pulling down into a frown, something Luke had never seen him do before.

"Charlie…"

He had that I'm-gonna-cry look on his face again, and Luke felt like crap for shooting him down. It was time Luke learned how to do what he was told.

"Okay, boys," he said, looking at the four eager faces turned up at him. "You need to spread your feet apart like this." Luke paused and stood still. Each little boy mimicked him, grins slapped on their faces. "Then you keep your arm stiff, bend and salute."

They were all following his lead and Luke had to try hard not to laugh. Such serious faces for a moment, then grinning and goofy the next. "Good work," he praised, internally kicking himself for being such a jerk when his son had asked him the first time.

Charlie kept hold of his legs, not ready to let go of his dad yet.

"You having a good birthday?" Luke asked him.

The boy nodded his head vigorously but still clung on. Tightly. The other boys had moved away and Luke wasn't sure what to do. Was Charlie hanging around so he could be with his dad? Was Luke meant to pick him up or would that be babying him?

From the corner of his eye he could see Ollie watching them still, and he had no idea what was expected of him.

So he did the only thing he could do, and went with his instincts. He scooped his son up high in his arms. "You sure you're all right, bud?" He tucked a finger under his chin to tilt his face up, but Charlie resisted for a moment, before turning his big brown eyes up to him.

"Charlie? Tell me what's wrong," he insisted.

"I don't want to share you," his son whispered.

Luke digested the words. If the boy hadn't looked so

serious he would have laughed. Didn't want to share him? As if he was some new toy he didn't want anyone else to play with?

"You don't share me, Charlie. I'm *your* dad, no one else's."

Charlie twisted his mouth and squirmed, before giving him a shy smile. Luke could see the confusion in his eyes.

"But I want you just for me, and Tom said he wanted a cool dad like you, too."

Luke was flattered, but he had a feeling this conversation was stemming from something deeper. Charlie no doubt already had issues about not having his dad around, and now that he was home, didn't like to think about Luke going away again. About losing him.

It scared the hell out of Luke to think a four-year-old could already have issues, problems, conflict in his mind. But there was no mistaking it.

"You know what? Why don't we go out and show your friends what playing soldiers is all about."

Charlie looked up at him, his eyes like saucers. "Really?"

"Yeah, or cops and robbers or something. Anything you'd like."

Charlie nodded.

"I'll be on your team, so you can have me all to yourself."

He dropped Charlie to the ground and followed him out. There was still a lot he didn't know about parenthood, but trying to make his son feel secure was a lesson he knew only too well. He'd had no one in his own life who cared enough about keeping him safe, but with Charlie, he could change that pattern. Had to change it.

Because otherwise he was just as bad as the foster parents who'd treated him like he wasn't worth the space he took up in their homes.

* * *

Olivia had an unfamiliar flutter tickle her throat. In all the time she'd been in charge of Charlie, been his number one, she'd never seen him look like this. Perhaps it was the party, maybe even the excitement of being that much older and enjoying his birthday, but deep down she guessed it was more serious.

Charlie was besotted with his father, that much was obvious, and it only made her fear deepen. It took hold with an iron fist inside her, and made her worry more than she'd ever known was possible. That dread within her that reminded her how quickly this could all disappear, how heartbroken her boy could be, with her left to pick up the pieces. She wanted so badly to push the thoughts away, to live in the now and take her husband for the man he was being right now. But being a mom changed everything.

Her son was her world, was her top priority in life, and seeing him so happy, so overawed by his father, only made her worry increase. It would affect him for the rest of his life to get to know his dad and then have him leave. And having him here at this age, knowing what it was like to have his dad at home, was worse than never knowing him. Charlie would never forget this time they'd spent together. Never.

Ollie looked up when she felt eyes upon her. Not just anyone's eyes, but the deep, dark eyes of her husband. She put down the knife she was holding, covered in chocolate icing.

"That's a good-looking cake."

She smiled. It was a great cake. But it wasn't the cake she was thinking about.

"Mmm-hmm."

She raised her head and Luke winked at her. It sent a

shiver down her spine even more delicious than the chocolate she was looking at.

"Need a hand carrying it?" he asked.

She nodded. "Please."

Luke moved toward her, his tall frame engulfing the small space. She was suffocated by his presence, like an insect caught in a spider's sticky web. Her feet were rooted to the spot, and although she wanted to move, to flee, memories of the night before kept her stuck like glue.

He brushed against her as he moved past, just the softest touch of his bare arm against hers. It made the tiny hairs prickle, her skin grow taut…and suddenly all she could think about was what they'd been doing in the kitchen barely twelve hours earlier. "We've got to stop meeting like this."

Luke paused before picking up the cake. "Am I doing okay?"

His question took her by surprise. "You're doing fine, Luke," she said. "Really fine."

He turned to her, his eyebrows forming a crease as he searched her face. "Really?"

She nodded.

"Because I feel like I could be making an idiot out of myself here and not know it."

Ollie tried not to laugh. She squeezed his arm, then ran her fingers lightly over his skin.

"We're doing okay, Luke. At least I think we are."

She braved a look, just one look at his warm, dark eyes. It was a mistake, but then she'd known that being in here with him again was dangerous. That she needed distance from him to avoid a repeat of losing control with him.

She opened her mouth to speak, but he shook his head, so slightly she could have been mistaken. Nothing seemed to move, yet he was closer to her, achingly close, and she wanted so desperately to have him against her. Last night hadn't been enough for her. Too much and not enough all at once.

Luke placed one finger to her lips, the roughness of his skin sending a shiver of pleasure like fireflies through her belly. She wanted him; she wasn't going to pretend otherwise. But the danger of it, the worry, made her want to run just as much.

"Luke, we need to take the cake in." Her voice was barely a whisper.

He smiled. "I know."

Ollie jumped a pace backward, her thighs connecting with the tower of presents stacked behind her. Luke was still watching her, not breaking that connection, but she felt the pull toward Charlie. Especially as she heard the squeals and shouts of the kids, just outside the room. It was his birthday, his special day, yet here she was, hoping Luke would jump her in the kitchen.

She gave him a half smile as her heart fluttered back to normal speed, her body was catching on to the fact that nothing was going to happen between them. At least not right now.

Luke picked up the cake, gave her another wink and headed out into the dining room. Ollie took a moment to compose herself before following him.

She didn't know what she was more scared of, playing happy families with Luke out there, or worrying about what was going to happen later, when everyone had gone. When they were alone, with no excuses.

CHAPTER TEN

CHARLIE BLEW THE candles out and Luke made a mental note not to sample any cake. He had a feeling that more spit had made its way to the icing than breath, and the little fingers inching closer to it made it seem all the less appealing.

He watched as Olivia knelt down beside the kids and started slicing pieces.

"It's a pretty good cake, huh?"

Luke turned to see Kelly standing beside him. "Yeah, doesn't look bad at all."

Ollie's friend smiled and moved closer. Luke wasn't quite sure if she was hitting on him or wanting to keep their voices down. He figured it was the latter, given how frosty she'd been the day before.

"How's everything going? Olivia hasn't mentioned how long you're back for."

So she was fishing for information. This was one thing he couldn't be beaten at, even if she tried to torture it out of him.

"It's great to be home." He took a sip of lemonade from his paper cup and wished it was something stronger. Something much stronger.

"Luke, I don't mean to pry, but I care a lot about Liv. She hurts, I hurt kind of thing."

Luke knew where this was going. He didn't mind being asked questions, but his wife was the only person he owed answers to. Especially when it was about *their marriage*.

"Look, Kelly," he said, turning to face her. "I appreciate your concern, and I appreciate that you've been a great friend to her, but this is between me and Olivia."

The woman smiled, but the angle of her head, the tilt of her chin, showed another emotion altogether. She wasn't going to let this go, he could tell.

"All I'm saying is that I don't want to see her hurt again. If you're not going to hang around, then maybe you should let her move on and find someone who will." Her words were cool. Clearly she had no problem telling him exactly what she thought of him.

Luke bit back the reply he wanted to give her, refusing to make an enemy of one of Olivia's closest friends.

"Just think about it, Luke." The sweet smile was back on her face as she composed herself and turned to walk away. "Nice to see you again."

He didn't bother to reply. Where the hell did she get off, approaching him at his son's birthday party and confronting him like that?

He knew he'd made mistakes. The very fact that he'd left, and in some warped way thought he'd done Charlie a favor, was the biggest of them all. But he'd come home for his son, and now he wanted Charlie *and* Olivia. The more time he spent here, the more sure he was.

"Luke?"

He turned slightly and saw Olivia standing beside him, a plate of cake in her hand.

He smiled, snapping out of it. "Hey. That for me?"

"If you want it." She grinned. "It tastes great."

"If you like spittle and sticky fingers, you mean?"

She waved her free hand in the air. "Being a parent

means plenty of spit and germs. Try some. I promise you'll like it." Breaking off a piece of cake with her forefinger and thumb she held it out to him. "Go on."

Luke hesitated. But the waggle of her eyebrows and the look of the icing between her slender fingers made him give in to temptation. Besides, if being a parent meant getting over hygiene rules, then he'd best give it a go now, while he was trying to prove himself.

She leaned closer when he opened his mouth to taste the cake, and Luke fought not to pull her entire body close at the same time. But he stayed still, swallowing the cake, and watching as his wife licked the sticky icing from her fingers.

"Good?" she asked.

He nodded. "Yeah."

Over the din of children playing and the stereo blaring kids' tunes, the doorbell sounded.

"I'll get it. You keep an eye on the party," Olivia instructed.

Luke watched her go, then tore his eyes away to focus on Charlie and his little buddies. She looked so lovely— so soft, so feminine, *so touchable.* And he wanted her. God, did he want her.

But he couldn't shake off what Kelly had said, no matter how much he didn't want to believe her. If Olivia's best friend didn't think he was good enough for her, was he? Luke hated that he was second-guessing himself, but he couldn't help it.

"Charlie, look who's here!"

Olivia's voice rang through the room, and Charlie jumped to his feet. Luke turned to see who had come.

It took him a moment, but then he realized where he'd seen the face before. Smiling at him from the mantel of the apartment, that day they'd gone to see Olivia at work.

"Luke, come over here. There's someone I'd like you to meet."

Olivia stood next to the man, who was dressed in a black suit, tie neatly hugging the collar of his shirt. *Ricardo*. Did Luke really have to meet a guy who was interested in his wife?

"Luke?" Olivia called.

He forced his feet to move, refusing to portray anything other than confidence. But he'd hated him on first sight.

Ricardo smiled. Luke tried to do the same without looking like a wolf baring his teeth.

"Luke, this is Ricardo. My boss." Olivia beamed. "He just dropped by to give Charlie a gift."

"Hi," Luke said, extending his hand. "Nice to meet you."

"I've heard a lot about you, Luke. Great to finally put a face to the name," Ricardo replied.

Luke nodded. He couldn't say he was pleased to be doing the same. Thankfully, Charlie started to rip into the paper on the large present he'd just received.

"Charlie!" Olivia scolded.

Ricardo smiled and placed a hand on Olivia's arm. Luke bristled, like a hedgehog about to be attacked. What the hell was he doing, touching her? *Was* there something going on between them?

"Let him rip. It's all part of the fun," said Ricardo.

Luke tried his best not to punch the guy. Instead, he let his fists curl at his sides. Was this what Kelly had been insinuating? That he should walk away for good and let Olivia move on with Ricardo?

Over his dead body!

"Cool!" Charlie was waving a massive dinosaur toy and a remote control.

Great, Ricardo had even managed to upstage Luke in the gift department.

"Glad you like it."

Charlie ran off to show his friends and Luke stood his ground. He had an instinctive feeling that he had to be the alpha male and stake out his territory. Show what was his and make sure the other guy knew it.

Olivia looked uncomfortable. She'd moved away from Ricardo to stand between them, but it wasn't enough. It was clear from the way Ricardo looked at her that he was in love with her. Did she honestly not see it, or was she trying to hide something?

"So what's it like to be home?"

As Ricardo spoke, Luke moved closer to Olivia. He looped his arm around her waist. "Great. It's great to be back with my family."

Olivia squirmed, but Luke held her firmly. He had no intention of letting her go until the jerk had left their home.

"Charlie's loved having his dad home," Olivia said, giving him a slightly confused smile. As if she wasn't exactly sure what he was doing.

"I'll bet he has," Ricardo replied.

"And thanks for the gift. It was far too extravagant, but Charlie clearly loved it," Olivia said. "Thanks so much for coming over."

"Yes, well, I'd better be off. Nice to meet you, Luke. See you next week, Olivia."

"You're going already? Stay for a coffee, some cake...." she suggested.

Olivia fought to get away from Luke's grasp so he let her go. His fingers bit into her skin as she pulled away and he wished he'd just released her, before she'd had to wriggle. He knew he was being childish, but he couldn't help it. This was his wife, his son's party, and he wasn't ready to have to fight someone else for what was his, not when he was struggling to keep hold of them as it was.

"I don't want to be in the way. I just wanted Charlie to have his present on his actual birthday."

"Well, it was very kind of you, wasn't it, Luke?"

She glared at him, as if she expected him to gush about the gift, too. "Yeah, thanks. Much appreciated," he managed to say.

Ricardo waved, glanced back one last time, then walked out the door. Luke had never been so pleased to see someone go.

Olivia waved goodbye then shut the door. She stood looking at the solid timber for a moment before turning slowly to face him. Luke went from slightly smug to feeling like an absolute idiot in two seconds flat.

"What the hell was that about?" Her voice was a low hiss, as if she didn't want anyone else to hear their exchange.

"What?" He didn't want to argue.

"You know what I'm talking about, Luke," she insisted, hands on her hips as she stared at him.

Jealousy and anger welled up in him, but he fought to keep his emotions locked away. All Ollie needed to know was that he cared, that he loved her.

"I don't know what you're talking about," he said, crossing the distance between them and reaching for her hand, trying to coax at least one of them from being planted on her hip.

"Luke, don't pretend nothing happened just then." Her voice was low and angry again, as if she was really starting to get mad.

"You mean the fact that your boss is in love with you?" He couldn't help it; she'd pushed him too far.

"What?"

She looked dumbfounded for a moment, before taking hold of his arm and marching him down the hall. He didn't want to cause a scene any more than she did, and he especially didn't want Charlie to see them argue.

"You're being ridiculous, Luke. Absolutely ridiculous."

Was he? "Just tell me the truth, Ollie. It'd be better than what's going through my head right now, what I'm imagining." Arguing like this was starting to remind him of the past, of before he'd left, and that wasn't a place he wanted to go back to.

"How dare you, Luke," she said, her eyes wide as she glared at him. "There is nothing, *nothing,* going on between us, and there never will be."

"I'm sorry. I had to ask." He was relieved, beyond relieved, to hear her say that. "But I don't think it's for his lack of wanting you."

From the look on her face, Luke was thinking he shouldn't have taken it any further. Should have just stopped talking.

"That's why you held on to me before, wasn't it? Some kind of stupid macho thing to try and tell him to back off."

Olivia marched within a inch of him when he said nothing to deny her statement.

"So that's what all this is about, huh? You trying to show what's yours."

Luke wanted to grab her. To kiss her, shake her, make things right. But he'd gone too far this time. Way too far. He should have just sucked up his pride and been confident in the knowledge that she was *his* wife. Instead, he'd managed to wreck things yet again.

"If you don't trust me, then this is over right now." Her voice was low, as if it was hard for her to say, but she was determined to get it out. "You can forget all about having a second chance here."

Damn. Didn't she know how hard this was for him? Wondering if he'd come back too late. Wondering if another man had already distracted her, when Luke had finally realized what an idiot he'd been to walk away from the one woman in the world who'd loved him.

"I'm not attracted to Ricardo, but he means a lot to me, Luke. He's been a great friend, and an even better employer. But that's *all*."

Luke bristled again, but this time kept his feelings inside. "I can't stand the thought of you being around him, not when it's so obvious how he feels about you. It's written all over his face." Luke sighed. "I trust you, Ollie, I promise I do. But I don't trust *him*."

She just shook her head, a sad look turning her mouth down into a frown. "You haven't earned the right to issue ultimatums, Luke."

Olivia turned on her heel and didn't look back as she walked away.

Anger like he'd never experienced before rippled through Luke. Not when he'd lost buddies on tour—never. Because he hadn't been able to control his jealousy, an emotion he'd never had to deal with before, and his wife had just walked away from him. She hadn't stayed to argue, she'd just stepped away, as if it wasn't even worth it.

He took a deep breath and walked back into the living room. *He needed to get out of here.*

Luke found Charlie and headed his way.

"Hey, bud, I've got to go out for a while. You keep having fun, okay?" he told his son.

Charlie looked up at him, smiled, then went back to playing. Luke straightened and surveyed the room before he left. He saw Olivia talking to another mom, her eyes trained on him.

But right now there was nothing left to say. He met her gaze for a moment, then turned and walked out the door.

Olivia watched Luke go. Just as she'd watched him go the last time, when he'd never returned.

Her eyes were dry this time, but it didn't surprise her. Deep down she'd known he would leave, she just hadn't expected it to be like this. Luke had never been the jealous type, but then, she hadn't taken him as the leaving type, either, and she'd been proved wrong there.

There had never been anything between her and Ricardo, but she had lied to Luke when he'd questioned her. Her boss had always made his feelings clear, had almost come close to proposing marriage, if her intuitions were correct. But even with the offer of financial security and complete stability, she would never go there. Because she didn't intend to marry again, not when she was still in love with her husband.

"You okay?" Kelly approached with a cup of coffee, slinging an arm around her.

Olivia braved a smile. Maybe she was wrong. Maybe Luke had just popped out for some fresh air? But she knew she was lying to herself even thinking like that. Because she'd seen the way he'd looked at Charlie, seen the sadness on Luke's face when he'd stood and watched his son, before walking away.

"I'm fine, thanks," she replied, nodding her head to convince her friend *and* herself.

"Nothing a good, strong coffee won't fix?"

Olivia forced another smile. "Exactly," she lied.

CHAPTER ELEVEN

AFTER ALL THOSE years of being away, of living rough, staying in places that he never hoped to see again, Luke had never thought he'd be bunking down in a shabby motel in his hometown.

He'd hardly expected Olivia to be waiting for him like a dutiful wife, because he knew he didn't deserve that kind of a homecoming. But he had expected to have a home. Even if only temporarily, until he figured things out.

Luke booted up the computer and sat back, deep in his seat, eyes shut tight. The memory of arguing with Ollie played through his mind, impossible to shut off, impossible not to regret. He could see the hurt, the sad slant of her eyes as she looked back at him. He remembered how choked her voice had been as she'd stood up to him.

Damn it! Why did he always have to mess everything up? The only thing in his life he was consistently good at was his job. Everything else he seemed to fail at miserably.

Luke could still see her boss standing there, looking so at home. Watching Charlie, *Luke's* son, as if he meant something to him. Giving him presents as if…as if he were his father. Luke swallowed hard, then gripped his fingers tight around the chair. Maybe if Kelly hadn't given him a dressing-down he wouldn't have reacted, but she had, and he'd taken the bait.

He'd felt threatened. He was jealous that this man, this Ricardo, might like to be Charlie's dad—had been acting like Charlie's dad while Luke was gone. And he'd flown off the handle, when what he should have done was stand up and be a man. Prove that he'd come home to reprise his role as father and show that he meant it. By not walking away.

Instead, he'd done the exact opposite.

His entire career had been about no emotion and absolute control. He thought he'd been doing it so long that it was a natural part of his life. But the tears falling down his cheeks proved he was wrong.

He kept his eyes squeezed shut for another few seconds, then opened them again, though he could barely keep them open. The pressure to try and fit in with the family he'd left, impress his kid, reconnect with his wife, had been making sleep almost impossible.

Luke forced himself to snap out of it. Exhaustion was traveling on foot for days on end with only one bottle of water and no food. Tired was when you had nowhere to sleep, no spot to lay your head. When you were constantly trying to stay one step in front of an enemy.

He sat up straighter and tapped in his log-in details. Eight new emails. Not bad, considering he hadn't checked for a few days. Luke scanned the one from Fort Bragg and felt a weight lift from his shoulders as the words lit up on the screen in front of him. *Wow.*

It was everything he'd ever wanted, the opportunity to make a difference, to be the soldier he'd trained all his life to be. But there was more to think about than just what he wanted right now, wasn't there?

He read the email again.

Mr. Brown, in recognition of your successful missions within your Special Forces Unit, we would like to discuss with you a new leadership opportunity. This would involve imminent redeployment, which we note that you have shown interest in volunteering for.

Luke skipped to the last line, read it slowly this time. Needed the words to sink in.

You have been offered this promotion due to your many deployments overseas, and the overall contribution you have made as part of your exemplary service to the United States Marine Corps. If you could phone to arrange a telephone conference or meeting at your earliest convenience, it would be much appreciated.

Could *he do it?* An image of Charlie playing with him in the park, smiling up at him, flashed through his mind. Charlie crawling into bed with him, warm body pressed to his, calling him Daddy.

But Charlie had to compete with Luke's equally vivid recollections of war, of his time in the Special Ops. Of the men he would be leaving behind, of the friends, *brothers,* he might never see again if he didn't take this opportunity.

He'd come home to be a dad, to reclaim the only family he had, but now the reality was tearing him apart. The division between right and wrong blurred beyond the point of recognition. He'd never intended to leave the army for good, but since he'd been home it was all he'd been able to think about.

He loved his wife. He'd thought she'd become like a fantasy in his mind, that the reality of her when he returned would be far different. But he'd been wrong.

But even if he didn't have a chance with her anymore, and God knew he didn't deserve one, he was still a father.

And it meant he couldn't just say yes, no matter how much he wanted to. If he went back to Delta, well, he might spend another couple of years away. Perhaps less, but it would still break that bond he was so slowly starting to develop with his son. Yet if he didn't take this promotion, what would he do? What would it mean if he gave up everything he'd worked so hard for?

Luke looked around at his surroundings—the yellowed walls, stained carpet and plaid bedspread. What the hell was he even doing here?

He grabbed his beat-up, old leather jacket and slipped it on, then left the room. He hadn't had a clear head for over three years, and now was the time to try to get one.

And if he stayed there any longer, he knew it might prove impossible to *not* pick up the phone and accept the position.

The streets seemed empty, but Luke wondered if he just wasn't taking everything in. His feet walked on autopilot, propelling him forward, without his mind telling them where they were heading. It was odd, walking aimlessly. On duty, he'd never walked anywhere without a plan, never made a move, a decision, without thinking through the logistics first. He pressed his thumb to his temple, trying to erase the memories that were held so tightly in check. Sometimes it was easy to push them back, to focus on something else and force them away, but not today.

He kept seeing his buddy lying there, blood sputtering out of him as he took his last breaths. They'd been together for such a long time, but in the end, when they were so close to achieving the goal, succeeding in their mission, his friend had been killed and Luke had been the one to come home.

The thought sent cool ripples of anger firing up and

down his body. It was so unfair. But if it hadn't happened—if he hadn't held his comrade in his arms as he took his last breath, listened to him cry that he would never see his child again—would Luke have been so quick to come home?

He wondered what Olivia would think if she ever saw his scars. Saw the jagged lines of wounds on his legs, or the scars crisscrossing his stomach. Could he tell her that he'd almost died? That fulfilling his duty as a soldier wasn't enough for him, that he wanted to succeed in her eyes, and for Charlie, too?

"Lieutenant Colonel Brown!"

Luke's head snapped up. He hadn't been called that since the day he'd touched down on U.S. soil.

"Lieutenant Colonel!"

He saw him then. A young man on crutches, hobbling out of a café on the corner he'd just passed. The face was familiar, but the name just didn't come to him.

Luke moved toward the man, conscious that he had both his legs working and the other man didn't.

"Lieutenant Colonel Brown," he said, dropping a crutch and holding out his hand. "Private Sam Roberts. I served under you my first tour in Iraq."

The penny dropped. Of course, his first deployment after Charlie was born, before he'd come home and then left for the Delta tour. Luke took his hand and shook it.

"Roberts. Of course I remember you." Luke smiled at the boy before him, pleased to see he'd made it home alive. "You back for good?"

"Yes, sir. My leg's busted up pretty bad."

Luke looked down, but then diverted his gaze. At least the boy had his legs. He'd seen far worse.

"And you, sir? You back now for a while?"

Luke swallowed what seemed like a rock. He'd thought

so, but was "home for good" ever going to be something that could describe him?

"I've been offered a position at base, but I'm still deciding."

"You would volunteer to go back there?"

Sam seemed unbelieving, and Luke didn't blame him. He was referring to Iraq, of course. He'd done his time, come home injured, but Luke? Well, he had something to prove, always had. Standing down wasn't something that was easy for him, even when the stakes were high.

"Let's just say I don't like leaving my boys over there without me."

He didn't tell him that Sam had been Delta Force these past two years. That if he'd run into him during that time he wouldn't have recognized him, would have walked right past him.

"Sir, I'd love you to meet my family. My fiancée and baby girl, they're just back there."

He pointed and Luke looked in that direction. The last thing he wanted was to make small talk when he needed to clear his head, but the boy was pretty enthusiastic.

"What do you say we take a rain check on that?" suggested Luke, smiling as he said it so as not to disappoint him. "I've really got to be somewhere."

He watched Sam's face fall.

"Give me your phone number and I'll come see you when I've got my boy with me. How old is your little girl?"

The young man's face lit up again. "She's two, almost two," he said. "Sir, I didn't know you had a family!"

Luke nodded. He'd always been reluctant to talk about his home life, so clammed up when conversation came to him personally. Yet here was this boy, so proud of his only child that it made Luke feel like an idiot. Or even more of an idiot than he had before.

"Charlie's four," Luke told him. "Great kid."

Sam beamed. "Yeah, makes coming home worth it, huh?"

Luke needed to go. Right now. It was as if just talking to this young man, barely twenty-one, had made him realize what a fool he'd been. That walking out on Olivia and leaving his boy wondering where he was had been stupid. Ludicrous. Luke couldn't blame this on his lack of upbringing; his behavior had been inexcusable. And he couldn't even think about taking the promotion without carefully thinking through the consequences, no matter how badly he wanted it.

"Hey, I gotta go. I'll find you through the database."

"But…"

He ignored him and started jogging, his feet thumping rhythmically on the pavement. Luke threw a hand in the air and waved, taking a quick look over his shoulder. "I'll phone you," he called out. "I promise."

He settled into a comfortable pace and focused on getting back to Ollie's place. *Their* place. It was at least a half hour run from where he was, but that was nothing. He was trained to jog for hours, on no food or water, in the desert. This was like a slow warm-up round.

His leg and side twinged a little, but he ignored it. It might have been enough of an injury to allow him to come home, but it wasn't enough to stop him fighting for his family.

Charlie was his son, and Olivia was the woman he wanted, and nothing was going to stand in his way. *Nothing.*

Twenty-five minutes later Luke stuffed his hands into his pockets and slowed to a walk. He hadn't found the run that bad, but didn't want to turn up puffing and sweaty, so decided to walk the last few blocks.

Part of him felt like an idiot—like an overreacting moron—but another part felt justified. That he'd had every right to fly off the handle and walk out. Although that part of him was dwindling. Fast. The more he thought about it, the more conflicted he was. The bravado of earlier had left him, to be replaced with a dull thud of worry that perhaps he might not be good enough. That he'd left it too long to say he was sorry.

The house stood before him. It was just a plain, modest bungalow, but it looked loved. Charlie's bike was out on the front lawn, dropped as if he'd been riding it, then found something better to do. A much-loved toy sat on the doorstep, from the looks of it a rabbit with long, floppy ears. It was like a snapshot of domesticity, and Luke felt a longing to be a part of it. A desire that had been dormant within him for so many years that he'd become afraid of claiming it.

He stood at the bottom of the steps and caught his breath. He was no longer panting from the run, but from the thought of what he had to say. How he would confront Olivia. He took one final lungful of air and moved to the door.

The house was quiet. No sounds emerged from within, though it seemed a little early for Charlie to be in bed, even if he was exhausted from the party. Luke tried the front door, but it was locked. He knocked, waited a few minutes, then knocked again. Perhaps they were out in back and couldn't hear him? It seemed unlikely.

He moved around the side of the house, navigating the trash can and an assortment of Charlie's outdoor toys, and peered in the window. Nobody there. He hoped they weren't out with Ricardo. Had Luke been so unreasonable that he'd pushed her away and into the arms of another man already? He clenched his teeth, swallowing his anger, the only evidence of it left in his hands, clenched into fists at his sides.

Maybe he'd come back in the morning. He had his wallet and the clothes on his back, and he could always wait until tomorrow to beg Olivia's forgiveness.

But his feet kept walking. Something niggled at him. A touch of worry played through his body, and he had a feeling that something wasn't quite right.

The back door came into view and he walked toward it. Through the pane of glass he saw Olivia. *She was there.* As if knowing he was near she looked up, and his stomach turned in a flip. The whites of her eyes and pained expression on her face told him something was wrong. That something was *very* wrong.

"Luke!" She screamed his name as if she was fighting for her life.

And that's when he saw Charlie.

She wasn't fighting for her own life, but for their son's.

CHAPTER TWELVE

FEAR GRIPPED HIS THROAT and threatened to strangle him. Luke seemed to move in slow motion, his shoes filled with lead, his legs working hard to keep up with his mind.

Charlie.

His limp, lifeless frame hung from Ollie's arms like a figurine. His little head lolled back, blond hair sticking damply to his forehead.

Luke fought to get through the door, his hands fumbling for the knob. He had to get control of himself. This was his *son*. This was *Charlie*. Luke stopped for a beat, no more than a second, and pushed his mind into work mode.

His job was to deal with critical situations, to save men and get them back home. Safe. *Alive*. This was exactly the same. He needed to focus, take charge and save a life. It was nonnegotiable.

But if he'd accepted that job offer, not come home when he did...

"Ollie," he called. The door was locked, and he only had one other option to get in.

Her eyes were wide, wild, unbelieving.

"Olivia!"

When she didn't do anything he yanked off his sweatshirt, wound it around his fist and smashed the window glass. He was beside her before she even seemed to register how he'd gotten in, and he moved fast to take Charlie into his own arms.

"Olivia!" he commanded. "Focus. Talk me through what happened."

He carried Charlie into the living room and placed him carefully on the sofa, his hands tracing a pattern over his son. Touching his face, chest, pulse, all the critical steps. He tried to ignore the pained expression on his boy's face, or the unnatural glaze in his eyes. He was alive, and that meant Luke had time to do something.

"Charlie, Charlie, stay with me, buddy."

Olivia fluttered beside him, her hands limp at her sides, as if she had no idea what to do.

"His inhaler did nothing. I called the ambulance but…"

Wait. Inhaler? "He has asthma?"

She nodded. "Yes, he…"

"Olivia, listen to me," Luke ordered. This he could handle. Asthma was something he could work with. "Get me the spacer."

She looked at him, her eyes empty, her skin pale.

"The nebulizer?" Please, God, let her have *something* for him to use.

"We don't have either. This hasn't happened before. It's never been bad like this." She started to cry. "I should have been more persistent with the doctor, but they said I didn't need to have anything other than an inhaler at home."

Luke let his mind work through the steps, thinking fast and logically. *He could make one himself.*

"Get me a paper cup and a knife."

She looked at him but didn't move.

"Now, Olivia. I need you focused."

She jumped into action.

"How long till the ambulance gets here?" he called.

"It should be here by now," she yelled back.

He knew they didn't have long. That asthma attacks of this kind were serious and required immediate care. He cradled Charlie's head and started rubbing his chest in wide, circular motions. His son seemed so small, so fragile, so weak. Luke didn't know what time the attack had started, but guessed Olivia had called the ambulance straight away. Every second, every minute counted. He knew that firsthand.

"What's happening? Can I help?" Olivia's voice lacked its usual strength. He wished he could comfort her, but he had to stay focused on what he was doing. She passed him the paper cup and inhaler.

"He's suffering from acute hyperventilation, it's a serious attack. He's not getting even fifty percent of the oxygen he needs to breathe."

Luke heard Olivia sobbing as she touched their son, but he kept his attention on Charlie. He took the paper cup and cut a hole in the bottom, then placed the inhaler through the hole.

"The more panicked he gets, the worse it will become, so I need you to stay calm, to talk to him." Luke paused, moving slightly so she could kneel beside him. "How many times did you try his inhaler?"

"Uh, he took maybe four puffs, but he struggled, and I don't know much he got. He usually only needs two when it's bad."

Luke nodded. "Charlie, I need you to listen to me. I'm going to make you feel better, buddy. You can trust me."

Charlie was wheezing and heaving, his body crying out for air.

"I need you to feel my hands on your chest. They're going to help you breathe. Think about how much fun we had at the park the other day and breathe slowly, in and out. In and out. Just keep thinking *in and out* as you try to breathe."

Luke started to coach him, tried to get him thinking about his breathing, and listening. But Charlie couldn't hear him, it was obvious. His little chest was struggling with the pain of each labored breath—short, choppy gasps that weren't putting enough air into his lungs.

"I need you to take a big breath when I puff this, ready?"

Luke placed the paper cup over Charlie's mouth and puffed the inhaler. He kept doing it, counting out four puffs and then giving him a rest.

"We need to do this every five minutes until the ambulance gets here."

Olivia had calmed down. She was cooing to Charlie in her most soothing tone.

Luke knew Charlie's pain. It was the worst kind of distress a human could experience, the feeling that you could no longer breathe. Knowing that there was nothing you could do but struggle to fill your lungs with the air they craved.

And he should know. He'd almost died from an asthma attack when he was a kid, only he hadn't had someone who loved him fighting to save his life.

The ghostly wail of a siren pierced Olivia's eardrums. For a moment she didn't know if it was real or in her imagination, until the flash of a red light ricocheted against the windowpanes.

It was as if she was in a dream, her legs taking too long to move, her senses heightened. All she could concentrate on were the labored breaths of her son, and Luke—his quiet words and strong presence the only thing keeping her together. *Keeping her sane.*

"Olivia, open the door."

She jumped to attention, resisting the urge to flee back to Charlie and take hold of him. The paramedics were rushing up the steps as she flung the door open.

"Please, come quick." The words came out in a jumble, but they pushed past her and moved inside.

Olivia followed them, feeling numb. Charlie's asthma had always been manageable. They used his inhaler when they needed to; he knew how to control his breathing; they went to the doctor regularly for checkups. So how had this happened? How had she come so close to losing her boy? If Luke hadn't arrived when he had... It didn't bear thinking about.

"He's stable. Good work," one attendant said.

Olivia watched the scene unfold. The female paramedic had her hands on Charlie. What was she doing?

"Luke, what are they doing to him?" Ollie's voice was strangled. Had he heard her? "Luke?"

Tears fell steadily down her cheeks as he took hold of her. Clasped his hands on her shoulders and drew her back to him, tight against his chest and safe in his arms. She'd thought she was stronger than this, that she could cope, but the pain in her lungs, in her heart, was almost suffocating. *Charlie was her baby and she'd almost lost him.*

"Ollie, it's okay. He's going to be okay," Luke soothed.

She twisted in his embrace, wanting to touch Charlie, to be there for him. But Luke held her firmly, not letting her interfere.

"Let me go! I need to be with him."

His hold tightened. "Let them do their job. He's going to be okay, Ollie. You need to trust me."

She wanted to believe him, but Charlie looked so lifeless, so fragile. His little body still heaved with every breath, as if he was still fighting to stay alive, only now he wore an oxygen mask.

"We need to get him to the hospital now, so they can administer a steroid shot. You can both ride in the van with us."

Olivia nodded. Luke let her go, but held her hand firmly with his.

"Come on," he instructed.

She leaned into him, letting him take her weight as they walked. It was like a dream, totally unreal. She'd been doing okay, thought she had the situation under control, but Luke, well, he'd been the hero.

He pulled her up into the ambulance and sat her down next to Charlie's head. Olivia placed her palm on her son's tiny arm, her other hand still gripping Luke's.

"It's going to be okay. We're over the worst of it," he told her.

His words comforted her, but her heart was beating a bit too fast. Her bones felt as if they'd turned to liquid and her head was pounding.

"You're the boy's father?"

Olivia looked up as the paramedic riding in the back with them spoke.

"Yes." Luke responded, his eyes never leaving Charlie's face.

"You did good back there. Where did you learn to deal with an asthma attack like that?"

Olivia watched Luke, but his face gave nothing away. She'd guessed his training made him good in crisis situations, but he *had* been pretty clued in about what Charlie was going through.

Luke glanced up for a beat and smiled at the paramedic. "Good army training, that's all."

Olivia looked from Charlie to Luke, trying hard not to

cry. It was so much to deal with, so much to cope with in a day. But there was one thing she couldn't stop thinking about, one thing she couldn't push away.

She still loved Luke.

And it wasn't just because their son could have died if Luke hadn't come home when he did. It was because she'd missed him like crazy while he was gone, regretted every argument, every angry word they'd said to one another. And now she was ready to actually think about that second chance he'd been so desperate for. The one she'd said she'd consider, but deep down hadn't really opened up to.

Well, now she was ready. She didn't care about his burst of jealousy earlier, she just cared about *him.*

"Ollie, he's going to be fine. You know that, right?"

Luke slung his arm around her shoulder, squeezing her close. She pushed in tighter to him, wishing he'd leave his weight there forever. Because Luke made her feel safe. He always had.

She smiled up at him, let her head fall into the crook of his arm. "I know."

When he dropped a kiss to her forehead she didn't pull away. Olivia snuggled in closer, eyes on her son as they bumped down the road.

I love you, Luke. The words sailed through her mind and tore through her heart. *I love you so much. Please don't ever leave me again.*

The ambulance slowed and Olivia planted her feet on the floor to steady herself. Charlie had started to heave again, and she just wanted to get him inside and checked over properly.

"You ready?" Luke asked.

He gave her a tight smile and held her hand, pulling her to her feet so they could jump out as the doors opened.

They moved fast so Charlie could be slipped out and whisked straight into the hospital. She had that feeling of complete helplessness again, as if no matter what she did it wouldn't make a difference.

Olivia followed the paramedics with Luke by her side, but she never took her eyes from her son. Until Luke tugged her hand and she realized they were in front of the reception desk, with Charlie being rolled past and away from her.

"Are you with the boy?" the receptionist asked.

Olivia nodded. She was so numb she could hardly speak. "Y-yes."

Luke squeezed her shoulder and moved forward, taking the forms from the woman behind the counter.

"We'll need to get you to fill these out."

Ollie wanted to go with Charlie, not sit around filling in paperwork! "Where are they taking him? I need to be with him. *Please.*"

"Ma'am, he'll be just fine. A doctor will be looking over him already, and you can go in as soon as this is done."

Olivia tried not to glare. She knew it wasn't the woman's fault, that it was procedure, but she just wanted to be by her son's side. She watched as Luke scanned the forms and then started scribbling, fast. She'd never been more pleased to have someone with her. Dealing with everyday life was hard enough. She couldn't have dealt with this on her own.

"Medical conditions? Medication?"

She shook her head. "No other conditions. Just his inhaler."

Luke continued to tick boxes and write words that she couldn't see.

"Has he had an asthma attack like this before? Anything worth noting?" He looked up, his eyebrows raised in question.

"No."

Just reliving the moment, thinking about the asthma attack again, brought tears to her eyes. She knew her blubbering wasn't going to help, but it was hard holding it all in check. Being in the hospital, knowing Charlie was in some room down the never-ending corridor, smelling that sterile hospital smell…it was awful. The last time she'd been in a hospital was when Charlie had been born. Before that it had been holding her mom's hand and saying goodbye to her.

A fresh wave of tears hit and Olivia couldn't stop it as they dropped silently down her cheeks.

"Okay, we're done."

She sat still as Luke went back and handed in the forms. When he returned it was to offer her a hand up.

"He's in room 105. Let's go."

Luke didn't need to ask her twice. Olivia hurried after him, her sandals flip-flopping as she walked as fast as her legs would move.

He stopped outside a closed door and turned to face her, reaching for both her hands. He touched her knuckles to his lips.

"Ollie, we need to be strong for Charlie. He's already frightened, but he's through the worst of it."

Olivia closed her eyes for a heartbeat and turned his words over in her head. Luke was right. Charlie needed to see them okay, coping, so no more tears. No hysteria. They needed to be a team.

"I know." Her words came out as little more than a puff of air.

"We can do this, Ollie," he said.

Luke took her hand and opened the door with his other.

She sucked back her emotions and fought the bite of worry that gnawed in her throat.

Because right now, she had to trust her husband.

Charlie was awake. Luke had told Ollie not to cry, to sit tight on her emotions, but he was struggling to hold it together himself. On the brink of crying like he'd never cried in his life. Sobbing.

Charlie might be awake, but he didn't look good. Gone was the slightly tanned complexion; now his son was ghostly pale. His eyes looked tired, exhausted, and Luke knew only too well how that felt.

Even though it'd been years ago, he'd never forgotten the feeling of his worst asthma attack. The panicked sucking of air, not able to fill his lungs with oxygen. The terror of thinking you were going to die, to suffocate, and then blacking out....

But Charlie had people who loved him, were fighting to save him, whereas Luke had had only himself. Had suffered through it without anyone holding his hand or hoping he'd make it. And he'd been only nine years old.

He pushed the thoughts away, kept his memories buried, where they belonged. Instead, he focused on Olivia, stayed close to comfort her as she reached for Charlie then cradled him against her.

A nurse smiled their way, standing close to Charlie's bed. Luke was about to ask her what happened next when the door to the room burst open and a fresh-faced doctor appeared.

"You must be Charlie's parents."

Luke made himself smile and shake the doctor's hand.

"I'm Dr. Lewis," he said, standing next to Charlie. "I understand you worked on your son before the ambulance arrived?"

Luke nodded.

"Good work. You may well have saved his life."

Olivia folded Charlie even tighter in her arms, as if just hearing the words made her relive it all over again.

"Where from here, Doc?" Luke asked. He didn't want to discuss what might have happened if he hadn't come home when he did, about what it said about him that he'd almost wanted to take a promotion instead of toughing it out at home and being a dad.

The doctor picked up Charlie's chart before answering. "We'll need to keep him here overnight, but he should be ready to go home tomorrow, so long as all his test results come back normal." He studied the chart some more. "We'll send you home with a nebulizer, and he will most likely need another shot of steroids in the morning."

Olivia spoke before Luke could respond.

"What are the chances of this happening again?"

The doctor looked at both of them, then sat down on the edge of the bed.

"It's hard to say, but Charlie certainly has severe asthma. More serious than you or your family doctor probably realized. What triggered this episode? Well, it's hard to say. What we need to do is figure out a plan to manage his condition."

Luke knew there was no hard and fast rule. No easy answer. But he did know that he'd been easily as bad as Charlie, if not worse, and he'd managed to deal with his asthma, to live with it. As far as he knew, he'd never have made it as a marine if he'd admitted to his condition, but he'd done what he had to do and he'd made it work. Hadn't let it hold him back. Although his asthma had started to fade as he grew up.

"He does carry an inhaler, doesn't he?" the doctor asked.

Luke looked to Olivia. It was the first he knew about Charlie's asthma, so he couldn't answer for that.

"No," she said, touching a hand to her forehead. "I mean, I usually keep one in my handbag, but he's never been this bad before. *Never.*"

"From now on, you'll want to make sure he always has one with him. I'll consult with a specialist to make sure we have him on the correct dosage."

Olivia had silent tears falling down her cheeks again, but Luke kept listening, wanting to absorb everything the doctor was telling them. When he finally left and closed the door behind him, Luke moved to the other side of the bed, across from Olivia.

Charlie smiled up at him, but he looked so weak, so small and vulnerable on the big hospital bed. Luke took his hand, so tiny in his own. So pale against his skin.

"You were so brave tonight, Charlie," he told him.

Charlie's face filled with a touch of color and his smile grew wider, as if he was lapping up the praise, had already forgotten about why he'd ended up in hospital.

"You're a fighter, you know that?" Luke told him.

"Like you, Dad?" he wheezed.

Olivia grabbed hold of him when he spoke, as if it was a miracle he was even talking, let alone breathing.

"You would make any soldier proud, bud, you hear me?" Luke said.

Charlie closed his eyes again, but the smile that played over his lips gave Luke the boost he needed. What if he hadn't come back? What if he'd sulked over what had happened at the party and not gone home again? What if... He cringed, refusing to play that game. Because he'd learned on tour not to think like that. Not ever.

His little boy needed him. And for the first time since he'd come home, Luke finally felt needed. He'd saved his son, and unlike so many of the men he'd tried to rescue over the years, Charlie had survived. No blood. No putrid stench of death. Just his little boy tucked up under a blanket, safe and alive.

Almost losing his son was something he didn't ever want to experience again. And from the look on Olivia's face, she was feeling every ounce as drained as he was.

"Ollie, I'll be back in a moment," he told his wife, giving her a reassuring smile. "I just have to make a quick phone call."

The old Luke would have run. Would have said yes to any promotion offered his way, would have bolted when the going got tough. But that wasn't him anymore. The new Luke was a dad, then a husband and *then* a soldier. Because if he couldn't put his priorities in that order? Then he had no business being back here at all.

CHAPTER THIRTEEN

OLIVIA LOOKED UP as Luke, his hands full, backed through the door. She wanted to get up to help him but her legs were dead, her body like an iron weight that was just too heavy to lift. Her nose was the only thing up to the task of reacting. *Real coffee*. Not the machine rubbish she'd been living on these past few hours.

"He's asleep." Olivia kept her voice low, almost a whisper.

Luke passed her a take-out cup and grinned. "One skinny large latte, two sugars."

"Mmm, you're my savior." Even as she said the words, she knew they went deeper. After tonight, he *was* her savior—hands down, no question about it. Her knight in shining armor, complete with the white horse.

"He looks so peaceful. Like he's dreaming about something good." Luke sat down next to her, his leg touching hers. Denim to denim, thighs brushing.

"Luke, how did you know what to do today?" She'd been wanting to ask him for hours.

They were talking at a normal level now, no more whispering. Charlie was sound asleep and she doubted that beating drums would wake him.

When Luke didn't answer, she continued. She could tell from the way he suddenly avoided her gaze that there was something he wasn't telling her. That there was something else. Something she needed to know.

"Don't tell me it was in your army first aid training course."

Luke delayed by taking a sip of his coffee, but she wasn't going to let him stay silent. He'd saved Charlie's life, but his actions had been practised. He'd known precisely what he was doing. What he had to do.

"I got some practice when I was a kid." His tone was flat.

Olivia didn't get it. What did he mean by practice? "Luke, I don't understand."

He gave her a half smile, and she wondered if she'd missed something. Was she so sleep deprived she was missing what he was telling her?

"I have asthma, Ollie," he told her. "Or at least I did when I was younger."

Wow. How did she not know that? "I can't believe all this time I've never known. That you've kept it from me." But it made sense. Of course it made sense, when she thought back to how he seemed to know exactly what Charlie was going through, how he felt.

Luke shook his head slightly. "I mostly grew out of it, so it's no big deal."

He was lying. She knew it was a big deal, whether he wanted to admit it or not. "How did you even make it into the army with asthma?"

He stretched out his legs and placed his coffee cup on the floor. She could tell he was uncomfortable, but she wanted to know. Had to know. It affected her son *and* her husband, so the more she knew about it the better prepared she'd be.

"I almost died when I was a little older than Charlie," he said, voice low. "The doctors told me if the ambulance had come five minutes later I would have died waiting."

The force of his words shocked her. Who had looked after Luke when he'd been suffering, when he'd been rushed to hospital? Who had been there for him? Olivia gulped. "Was it just like Charlie?"

"Yup." The shrug Luke gave, the way he couldn't look at her, told her it was hard for him to be telling her about his past. "I know what it feels like to try so hard to suck in air and fail. But the difference is that Charlie had two people fighting for him to live, and I had no one."

Olivia had thought she was all out of tears, but she was wrong. Sometimes she forgot how bad Luke had had it as a kid, how much he must have suffered.

"What happened after that?" she asked in a choked voice.

Luke looked up at the ceiling, fighting what she could only guess was his own emotion. Olivia reached for him, touched her hand to his thigh and never took her eyes from his face.

"I had a great doctor and he helped me. Even kept me in the hospital for a few extra days because he could see what was happening," Luke told her. "Then I read up all I could, as much as I could understand at the time, and just decided to do everything I could to fight it."

"Like it was a disease or something? You were fighting the symptoms?" she asked.

Luke nodded. "I went from being a sickly kid who couldn't even run a block to the fittest kid in school, and I always carried my inhaler. That was when things changed for me."

Olivia was all ears. She'd never known that Luke was weak when he was younger. All she'd ever known was the fit, strong, athletic Luke. The soldier. *Weak* and *Luke Brown* were not words she would have ever strung together.

"I was bullied every day in foster care, picked on in class, made to sit out on activities because I couldn't catch my breath long enough to run. Then I learned how to breathe properly through my nose, how to control my asthma, followed alternative practices that a doctor had told me about." He shrugged. "It changed my life."

"Does the army know about your condition?"

Luke's eyes turned on her then, stormy and dark, as if she'd said something terrible to offend him. "All I know is that I set a record on the fitness test when I joined, and I've never had a problem. *Period*. As far as I'm concerned, asthma was something that used to control me, but I mostly grew out of it."

The door swung open then, filling the room with a bright, artificial light.

"He still asleep?"

Olivia turned and smiled at the nurse. "He seems to be doing great, thanks."

"If anyone knows how to beat this, it's me," Luke told her, covering Ollie's hand with his when the nurse had checked Charlie's condition and left again. "I'll teach him how to deal with it, trust me."

Olivia smiled at Luke and watched the stern lines of his face as he looked at Charlie. He was hard to read, one minute light and chatty, the next serious and deadly. But one thing she was sure about was that she was pleased to have him here.

Parenting was tough, and it was nice to have someone by her side for once. Especially since that someone was Luke.

They were lucky Charlie was such an easy kid. Luke looked in the rearview mirror and grinned at his son.

Olivia was riding in the back with him, babying him, and the boy didn't like it one bit.

"Mom!" He wriggled away and Ollie sighed.

"You've been very sick, sweetheart. I'm just trying to look after you."

Charlie rolled his eyes and squirmed some more.

"Mommy, you're embarrassing the kid." Luke was pleased he was in the front seat. Ollie glared at him as if she'd punch him given half the chance.

"Yeah, Mom, you're embaroosing me."

That made them both laugh. Charlie joined in, which made them laugh all the more.

Luke pulled the car into the drive and stopped outside the garage. He made it around to the other side in time to hear Ollie offer to carry Charlie. It didn't go down well.

"He's okay. You know that, right?" Luke asked her. "He doesn't have a life-threatening illness."

Ollie nodded, but she didn't look convinced.

"Let's get inside. Come on," he told her.

Luke couldn't help but think how different the house looked this time around. The last time he'd walked up the front path he'd been confronted by a silence that had worried him, and then he'd found Charlie. This time, his boy was waiting at the front door, wriggling on the spot. He sure didn't like to stand still for long.

"What's for dinner?" he called out to them.

Luke stifled a laugh. Typical boy. Playing and eating, that was all he thought about. *All a kid should have to think about.*

"Let's see," said Olivia as she unlocked the door and let them all in. "How about homemade pizzas?"

"Yay!"

"Luke?" she asked.

He put his hands in the air. "Fine by me."

"Come on then. Charlie, you can help."

Luke sat on a stool on the other side of the counter and watched the fun. Charlie was standing on a chair so he could help his mom, and there was food everywhere. Flour was smudged on Charlie's face, hair and the front of his T-shirt, and now he was trying to help spread sauce on the dough while Olivia cut up tomatoes, basil and peppers. The one Charlie was working on was a mini pizza, which he'd insisted only have ketchup and cheese.

"Are you sure you don't mind vegetarian?" Olivia asked.

Luke couldn't drag his eyes away from Charlie, who had his tongue between his lips as he concentrated. "Not at all. Whatever you make will be great."

"I usually make chicken pizza, but this is all I had in the fridge."

"Mine's cheese and ketchup," announced Charlie.

"So I see." As if he could have missed him demanding his choice of toppings before.

"It's his favorite," Ollie told him, still busy chopping. "I kind of give in when it comes to pizza. My theory is that he may as well enjoy it, especially if he's making it."

Luke liked that she was so concerned about healthy meals that she felt guilty about this one, but he didn't like that she always justified herself to him. She was a great mom and no one could fault her. Most certainly not him, especially after being gone for so long and leaving all the hard parenting to her.

"Charlie, how about you go wash up? I'll pop them in the oven." Olivia helped him down and he ran off down the hall as if his life depended on it.

"Luke, I need to thank you for what you did last night."

She wasn't looking at him, her hands busy sprinkling cheese over the pizza.

He shrugged. "It was no big deal." And it wasn't. Any man would have done the same for his child. Besides, she'd already thanked him.

Olivia looked up at him then, used her arm to brush away a few stray strands of hair as she locked eyes with him.

"It was a seriously big deal, Luke. You saved his life." She had tears in her eyes now. "It means everything to me that you came back, especially *when* you did."

He could see the emotion building up within her. Yes, he'd helped Charlie, but the ambulance had arrived fast, so he would have made it anyway. At least Luke hoped so. But thinking about what-ifs, thinking about what might have happened if he hadn't come back when he did, wasn't worth it. The only thing he was proud of right now was the fact he'd had the guts to turn down the promotion and ask for more time before he decided what to do next.

"I should never have walked out on the party, Ollie." And he should have apologized earlier.

"Luke, really, you don't have to say anything." She picked up the pizzas and slipped them into the oven, suddenly not able to meet his gaze.

"No, Ollie, it was wrong. You didn't deserve it. I, well, I just shouldn't have done it. I behaved like an idiot."

Ollie shook her head, took a few steps toward him and wrapped her arms around herself. "I forgive you, Luke. It's water under the bridge. You saved our son's life, so I'm hardly going to hold it against you."

It was as if something had changed between them. The smile on her face, the look in eyes… There was an openness there that he hadn't seen, not like that, since he'd returned. It was as if she was forgiving him for more than just one argument, giving him a fresh start. Had he read it wrong, or was she trying to tell him something?

"Olivia…"

She smiled at him. The most beautiful, open, genuine smile he'd ever seen. "I *forgive* you, Luke. I do."

All the pain of coming home, all the memories he'd held so tight, all the worries about what to do and how to behave, had all been worth it. That smile meant everything to him, her words the best melody he could imagine. Because now he might actually have a real chance with her. Not at a night with her, not at seeing how things panned out, but a chance at a *future*.

CHAPTER FOURTEEN

LUKE JUMPED TO his feet as the doorbell rang. He'd been playing trains with Charlie, building a track that took them right around the living room.

"Coming," he called.

The door was solid timber, so he couldn't see who was there. He pulled it open.

"Kelly." Luke said her name because he didn't know what else to say. He wished he wasn't home alone. The last thing he needed right now was a grilling about his behavior, or a lecture about what was best for Olivia again.

"Hi, Luke. Can I come in?" she asked.

He could hardly say no. "Of course."

Luke moved aside so she could pass, and then closed the door behind them. He would have preferred to step out and leave her in the house alone, but the last thing he needed was for her to have even more ammunition against him.

"You don't have your daughter today?" It was the only thing that crossed his mind to say to her.

"I've just dropped her off at her grandparents' place. They have her once a month for the weekend."

"Her dad doesn't see her?"

She shot him a look he didn't want to be on the receiving end of again.

"No." She emphasized the word more than was neces-

sary. "He walked out two years ago and I've hardly heard from him since. His folks make a big effort, though, so she has great grandparents."

Luke wished he hadn't asked. No wonder she and Ollie were such good friends. They both had husbands who'd walked out, and from the look on Kelly's face she might just hate the entire male population.

He groaned. There was nothing he could do to rectify the past more than be here right now, so there was no use beating himself up over it.

Charlie saved him, storming back into the room with his wooden gun.

"Bang, bang!"

Luke laughed and pretended to be hit. Kelly didn't look that impressed, but he wasn't going to stop playing with Charlie just because they had a visitor who might not be into weapons.

"Did you say hello to Kelly?" Luke asked Charlie.

"Hi, Kelly." Charlie repeated on autopilot, before running full speed at Luke. "I got you!"

Luke hoisted Charlie up into his arms before turning to face Kelly. "We've been having some boys' fun time, haven't we, big guy?"

Charlie nodded, then wriggled to get down.

"You go play with the trains. I'll be back to help soon," Luke told him.

"I hear you did pretty good the other night," she said.

"Coffee?" Luke hoped she'd take the hint that he didn't want to talk about it.

"Sure."

"Sugar?" he asked, heading for the kitchen.

Kelly shook her head. "Liv tells me you saved him, Luke. That without you it could have been a lot worse."

Luke didn't want to be the hero, because he was the one

who'd walked out on the party. *And that had been anything but heroic.* He'd hated the hero tag in the army, and he hated it just as much as a civilian. You just did what you had to do to save someone. It was what he was trained to do, and it was what any other human being would do in the same situation. Particularly for their own child.

"He's okay, that's the main thing."

Luke passed her a mug and she took it. He sipped from his own. The liquid was far too hot, but he continued anyway. Drinking scalding coffee was preferable to making small talk as far as he was concerned, even if he did lose all the skin on the roof of his mouth.

"Look, Luke, the reason I came around was to make peace with you."

He digested Kelly's words. So she'd known Olivia wasn't going to be here.

"She's told me that the two of you are trying to work things out, to make a go of it, and I want to help," Kelly said.

Olivia had actually told her that? "I don't understand what you're offering."

"Look, I don't have my daughter all weekend, and I have nothing else to do. Why don't you and Liv spend a day together tomorrow, just the two of you? Do something nice, go somewhere."

Wow. He sure hadn't expected that. "That's really kind of you, but I'm not sure."

Kelly sighed. "You need some time alone, without Charlie around. Stay away the whole weekend if you like, but just make sure you do *something.*"

Maybe she was right. The last thing he wanted was to leave his son, not when he was enjoying him so much. But a day or night away with his wife? Just the two of them?

"Charlie's only been out of hospital two days. I don't think Olivia will go for it," Luke stated.

"Don't think I'll go for what?"

Olivia stood in the doorway, her eyebrows arched in question. She had her arms folded, forming a barrier over her chest. And she didn't look impressed.

"Hey, Liv." Kelly put her coffee down and stood to give her a kiss on the cheek.

Olivia went through the motions, but still didn't look convinced.

Luke shrugged, trying to ignore the question.

"Don't think I'd go for what?" Olivia repeated.

Luke looked at Kelly, but she wasn't being any help. Damn it. This whole thing hadn't even been his idea, and he was the one undergoing the interrogation.

"Kelly has offered to look after Charlie if we want to spend some time together tomorrow," Luke told her.

She uncrossed her arms. At least she didn't look so angry now.

"I can't leave him." It sounded as if there was no room for changing her mind, but then Luke had expected that. "What if he had an asthma attack again?"

"He's not going to, Ollie. We've got everything under control," Luke assured her. "But I feel the same as you, so if you don't want to, I understand. He still coughed a lot last night."

"I…" She'd gone pink in the face, her cheeks flushed.

"You know you can trust me with him, Liv." Kelly got to her feet. "I'll leave you guys to talk about it, but I'm happy to help out. Just pick up the phone and I'll be here."

Olivia walked Kelly to the door and Luke stayed put. It *was* a good idea, he'd give her that. They needed to spend time together to see if there was any chance for them to ever go back to what they'd once had. He'd proved to her that he loved Charlie, and enjoyed every single moment in his son's company, even when things were tough. But for them to figure things out between them, to get their marriage back to a point where they could build a future? It was something that needed more than time to heal. It needed action.

Olivia walked back into the room and picked up one of Charlie's books. She held it in her hands before dropping it into a basket.

"I just hate the idea of leaving him," she said. "I've never left him. Not even for a night."

Luke walked toward his wife and stopped a few feet from her. He reached out and touched her arms, one hand to each of her elbows, wanting to be close to her but not wanting to push her, to crowd her if she wasn't ready.

"Why don't we go to Laguna Beach?" he suggested. "Lunch at a nice little restaurant, stroll past the shops, walk along the beach? We could just go for the day."

She slowly nodded her head, almost reluctantly. But he'd known she'd want to go there, because it was the place they'd first met.

"Is that a yes?" he asked, the corner of his mouth kicking up into a grin.

Ollie smiled back at him. He tried not to watch that smile, not to focus on her mouth, but it was hard. Those pouting, pillow-soft lips were tempting, but he restrained herself. He had to keep his desire in check, rein back on what he wanted. If she gave him another chance, there would be plenty of time for that. Right now he needed her to trust him.

"So we'd only be gone for five or six hours?" she asked.

"We could take our overnight bags just in case," he suggested.

Olivia shook her head fiercely. "Uh-uh. No."

He stooped slightly to look into her eyes, hands still on her elbows. "Just in case?"

"You're pushing it, Luke." She looked panicked now, as if the whole idea of leaving terrified her more than he'd even come close to understanding.

He stepped back. Surrendered. "Okay, we'll just drive there for lunch, take a few hours."

Her face softened and she started to smile again. "Deal."

Olivia found herself struggling to inhale enough oxygen when Luke went to find Charlie. There didn't seem to be enough of it in the room for her.

All she could think about was what it would be like to spend an entire day with Luke. Sit in a car beside him with no one else, no Charlie, to focus on. Just the two of them.

It was stupid to be nervous, but the thought of that made her worry. Made her stomach flip-flop, twisting in circles at the same time.

A date day. That's what it sounded like. But it seemed more like a first date, like she'd been waiting for him to ask her out her entire lifetime, or at least that's how the pressure building in her chest was making her feel.

Luke was the father of her child. She'd never intended on giving him a second chance, not after all this time, and now she was turning herself inside out at spending *one day* with him? She wasn't unhappy about how things were changing between them, but it didn't mean it was easy.

She heard Charlie squeal with delight and wondered what he and Luke were doing. It scared her, having Luke here. It had been one thing having him in the house when she'd thought it was temporary, but ever since that night in the hospital, things had been different. There was a slow fire burning beneath the surface, simmering between them. A fire that she wanted to keep stoking, but didn't want to let burn too hard. Or be extinguished.

She was so confused.

Luke had earned this opportunity. When he'd asked her that night, just after he'd returned, she'd said *yes* to him out of duty. Wanting to provide a family for Charlie, yet wary of the pitfalls of doing so. She'd still been attracted to Luke, very much so, but she'd had no true intention of letting him back into her heart. She'd thought that part of her was shut away.

But now? Now she was on the brink of opening herself up to him, of telling him she'd shred the damn divorce papers. It terrified her, but at the same time was exciting. And that's why a day away together was adding to her worry, because in that length of time she'd probably know whether they were ever going to give their marriage a true second chance.

It was time to let go of the past and see if they had a future.

CHAPTER FIFTEEN

A WHISPER OF almost-cool wind touched Olivia's cheeks and made her smile. Senses she'd once ignored, feelings she'd pushed back while Luke had been away, were all starting to return to her.

And the biggest sensory experience right now? *Luke.* One month ago, she would have said her wounds were too deep to ever heal, that the skin had only just sealed over what still hurt like a raw sore. But now fresh skin had grown, and she'd seen the man she'd once loved in a new light. As a possible dad to their son, rather than a long-distance no one.

As a rogue wave splashed over her toes, Ollie took a silent gulp of air and glanced at Luke. He smiled back, the kind of toe-tingling smile a teenage crush might give a girl, and it had the exact effect on Olivia that she was terrified of. Luke walked closer and reached for her hand. A simple touch that conveyed nothing and everything all at once, and made her toes curl deeper into the sand.

It was then that she knew she was lost to him. That despite all her protests, despite that shallow voice of doubt still urging her to resist, she was going to give him a second chance. A real, no-holds-barred second chance.

"You okay?" Luke asked her.

Olivia nodded. She didn't trust her voice not to wobble

if she tried to answer. Luke squeezed her hand and they started to walk, silent, yet more connected than they'd been in years.

"Do you remember this spot?"

She kept hold of his palm as Luke stopped and searched her eyes for her answer. Ollie looked around, slowly at first, then her gaze raced about them. Oh, yes, she remembered this place.

"Mmm-hmm." She searched for words and found none.

"I wasn't sure if you'd remember..." His voice trailed off and he dropped her hand.

Olivia forced her head up, trying not to blush at the dream she'd had about this exact spot when Luke had first arrived back. *This had been their beach, their place.* Where, like teenagers, they'd made love out in the open, in the dark, with only the roar of waves as their witness. It had been so unlike her, so out of her comfort zone, but it had been incredible.

"The night I fell pregnant with Charlie," she told him.

Luke looked into her eyes and Olivia forced herself to meet his steady gaze, not to shy away from his attention. *Because this was Luke.* Not the Luke who had deserted her, but the Luke she'd fallen in love with. The man she'd so desperately hoped would come back to her when things had started to become strained between them. When she thought she'd lost him forever.

"Do you regret it?" he asked, his voice low.

Did she regret Charlie? Absolutely not. Her *marriage?* She honestly believed that if given a choice, she'd rather say she'd loved and lost than never loved at all.

"No, Luke. I don't regret any of it." She took a deep breath. "Except for the years we spent apart, and the arguments we had before you left."

Luke brought his face nearer, eyes trained on hers. She

wanted so badly to flee, but more than that she wanted to feel his lips, to be lost in his kisses.

He paused, hovered, his mouth so close to hers. Olivia parted her lips, her breathing shallow, eyes almost shut.

"You don't regret me?"

She shook her head. *Never.* But there were things she'd have done differently.

It was obviously the response he wanted, what he'd been waiting for. Olivia stifled a moan as he closed his lips over hers, a soft press that had her aching for more, reaching out to hold on to him.

Luke circled his arms about her and pulled her close, one hand pressed firmly into the curve of her back. As the doubts tried to rise, tried to stifle what she wanted so badly to just enjoy, Ollie closed her eyes tighter, savoring the way Luke felt against her. What it was like to be in his arms again.

When he pulled back, he didn't let go, and Ollie stayed in place, feet planted in the sand. His eyes, brown and honest, stared straight through her, straight to her heart. She reached one hand to trace his face, over the stubble on his handsome jaw, then down his neck and to his chest. It was strong beneath his T-shirt, the cotton doing little to conceal his muscled frame.

"What do you say we stay here the night?" Luke asked, his voice husky.

His question almost took her more by surprise than his kiss had. "What about Charlie?" No matter how good this was, could she actually stay away for a whole night?

"Let's see how he's doing," said Luke, his voice barely more than a whisper as he spoke into her ear.

That deep, throaty voice was enough to sway her. Because if she said yes, then maybe they really could test the waters, see if they could make this work on every level.

"Okay," she agreed, before she could change her mind.

Leaving Charlie wasn't something she wanted to do, but if it meant a chance of Mommy and Daddy coming back home a couple again? She doubted he'd mind one night without them.

And maybe this time she'd believe that Luke wanted her, rather than thinking his actions stemmed from some deep-seated sense of duty.

Olivia ended the call and glanced at Luke. Charlie was fine and Kelly was happy to let him stay over, which meant Ollie had no excuse to change her mind. She looked out the window at the people going past, gazing out toward the water from the room they'd just checked in to.

A noise from behind made her turn. She instantly wished she hadn't. Luke was pulling his T-shirt off, exposing a serious set of abdominals and a tan to envy. She tried to look the other way, but her eyes just wouldn't obey her, and she could hardly blame them.

"Thought I'd better scrub up for dinner." Luke had a big grin on his face as he stepped out of his jeans, as if he knew exactly what he was doing to her, teasing her like that. "Because I'm guessing he's still doing fine?"

Olivia gulped. It was like trying to swallow an apple. Whole. So she'd phoned home twice already. She was a mom; what did he expect?

Before she could say anything he walked into the bathroom, wearing only his boxer shorts. The next thing she heard was running water, and steam came billowing out the door a few moments later.

Olivia took the chance to tidy herself. She wound her long hair up into a loose knot, fiddling with some shorter pieces at the front. She pulled some makeup from her handbag and reapplied her foundation, lipstick and mascara.

"You look beautiful."

Olivia looked up into the mirror. Luke was standing in the doorway to the bathroom.

"Thank you."

He scrubbed at his head with a white towel before tossing it back into the bathroom. Another towel was tucked low around his waist, meaning she got another eyeful of his body. A tingle ran through her again, telling her that no matter how much she wanted to be careful, to make sure she wasn't hurt again, saying no to Luke wasn't going to be an option. Not with his body on display in front of her, reminding her just how much she'd enjoyed being with him...

"What do you say we have fries and calamari down the road, just like old times?"

Olivia nodded, dragging her eyes away from him. "Sounds good to me." And it would give her longer to swallow some more of her fear.

She turned as Luke dressed. It wasn't as if she'd never seen him naked, but she didn't want to ogle him quite that openly yet.

"We're going to have a great time tonight, Ollie." Luke dropped a kiss on her head as he passed, fingers skimming her shoulder as he took the towel back into the bathroom.

Tonight. It was a loaded word, could mean so much, and that's what terrified her. And excited her at the same time. Because she had no idea whether they'd end up talking about the past over dinner, or lying on the beach in one another's arms again.

Luke stood near the door. "Ready to go?"

She rose and took the hand he offered her. "I think I can already taste those shoestring fries and aioli."

Olivia interlaced her fingers with her husband's and tried not to think about how hard it would be to lose him again. When she'd finally accepted him back into her life. When she'd finally opened up to trusting him again.

The sun had started its descent, but fluffy clouds hid it from view. The wind had a hint of coolness, but then Olivia thought she was probably oversensitive right now. Luke had his eyes trained ahead and she couldn't stop watching him.

His face had been ingrained in her memory for so long. She'd spoken to other army wives who'd worried they would forget the memory of their husband's faces, but that was never something that had concerned her. It seemed as if every day, week, month that had passed made her remember Luke more vividly. As if he was a constant presence in her life rather than an absent one.

The breadth of his shoulders, even from side on, the curve of his dark eyebrows, the length of his eyelashes. They were things she would never forget, and yet had hoped so hard sometimes that she could. The memory of him had made every other man she'd met since unappealing, and yet the reality of him had, until now, disappointed her more than she could ever have imagined.

Luke. She breathed his name through slightly parted lips. *Her husband*. Would he still be her husband next week, next month? It seemed an age ago that she'd demanded he sign the divorce papers, and she wanted so badly for him to tell her he was going to stay. For good this time. But she was too scared to ask, didn't want to know, because she didn't want anything to cloud her judgment or the way she was feeling about him. What was developing between them.

"I think we're both a little lost in our thoughts."

Olivia turned her gaze back to Luke and nodded. "That could have to do with how beautiful it is here."

He leaned closer and slung his arm around her shoulders. "Thinking about Charlie?"

She shook her head. "Funnily enough, no."

"I was," he admitted.

She would never have guessed, had expected him to be thinking about war. "What about Charlie were you thinking?"

"How lucky he is to have a mom like you." Luke turned to face her, his eyes looking straight into hers, not letting her glance away. "You're a great mom, Ollie, and Charlie's a lucky boy. I just hope that one day he can say the same about his dad."

Ollie smiled even though tears flooded her eyes. "He's always been proud of you. Told everyone everything he could about his dad who's away at war. I guess you just have to live up to the hero he's created."

"No pressure, huh?" Luke grinned.

"Oh, there's plenty of pressure!"

They both laughed and started to walk again. The little place they planned to eat at was just ahead. "Come on," Luke said.

And when he put his arm around her this time, she fell into his embrace and let her head touch his shoulder. Because it was where she wanted to be. Snug under her husband's arm, rid of the memories of being left, and with a real chance at a future. Now she just needed to trust in him when he told her how he felt.

From across the table, Luke watched his wife. It was a word he'd said over and over in his mind when he'd been away. *Wife.* He knew he had one, but it hadn't seemed real. From the moment he'd shipped out, it was as if the life he'd had for such a short time as a civilian had disintegrated. He'd been a soldier for most of his life, created a family for himself there, and the loyalties he had were so conflicted. Ollie was everything he'd ever hoped for. Sweet, kind and fiercely loyal. *And that face.* It had been her eyes he'd noticed first, from across the bar, where she'd sat laughing with girlfriends. Luke had abandoned his mates without a backward glance to go talk to her, and the rest was history.

Even now, he couldn't explain how they'd managed to let their marriage fall apart as it had, and he was done with blaming it on his past. Yeah, he'd lost his parents, and foster care had been tougher than hell. But he and Ollie had had a good thing, only he hadn't been able to convince his wife that he hadn't just married her because she'd been pregnant. Because the truth was, he'd never wanted children, and he'd made the mistake of telling Olivia that… before she'd told him she was carrying his child.

"What are you thinking about now?" she asked him.

Luke jumped out of his thoughts and into the present. "You. Charlie. Everything."

She smiled back at him, her eyes shining. This honesty thing was easier than he'd thought.

"Are you pleased you're back here?"

He placed his beer bottle down and touched her hand across the table. "More than you'll ever know."

Ollie giggled. Luke looked down at his hand. Salty and greasy from the fries, not exactly romantic.

"We used to have fun, you and me. Before things went and got all complicated."

She grinned and passed him a napkin. "I think we still do. Have fun, that is."

He watched as she ate another fry, before pushing her plate away.

"I'm done." She'd hardly left a scrap on her plate.

"If I didn't know you better I'd say you hadn't eaten in a while."

It had always been a joke between them, how much food the girl could eat without putting on a pound.

"You know me," she teased.

Luke caught her eye. He had once known her so well, and he almost, *almost* had that feeling back again.

"I know I've said it before, Ollie, but I need you to know how sorry I am for what happened between us. For the way I left."

He watched as she swallowed, fingers twitching beneath his. "I know you are, Luke. I believe you." Ollie hesitated. "And it wasn't just your fault. I can't keep blaming you and acting like it was all your doing."

"Ollie, I'm the one who left."

"Yeah, but who pushed you into it, Luke?" She had tears in her eyes now, which she brushed away, and he squeezed her hand again, laced his fingers tight around hers. "I know I was to blame, and I need you to hear me say it."

"Let's just say that neither of us helped things, huh?" he suggested. The last thing he wanted was for her to be hurting when they should both be feeling more positive. "I…" He cleared his throat, made himself tell her what he'd held back for so long. "When I told you I didn't want children, I never told you why, and I've wished all this time that I'd at least tried to explain myself."

She laughed. "You mean before I jumped down your throat and told you I was pregnant?"

Luke lifted his shoulders in a shrug. "Something like that." He looked away and then back at her. "When my parents died, I was old enough to remember them, and it made everything I went through so much worse, because

I knew how different things would have been if they'd still been here."

Olivia grasped his hand tightly.

"When I decided to become a soldier, I also decided that I never wanted to be a dad. Because I knew how dangerous my job was, and I didn't ever want a child of mine to experience what I had. I didn't want them knowing what it was like to have a dad, then lose him, and when I knew I was being redeployed, part of me honestly thought that Charlie would be better off not knowing me."

"Oh, Luke!" Olivia was shaking her head. "I hope you know that's not true. And all the things I said, how sleep deprived we were with a difficult baby at the time, and me thinking I'd somehow trapped you into a marriage you didn't want…"

"It's not your fault, Ollie." He took his hand from hers so he could pick at the label of his beer bottle. "I still could have come back, tried to make things better, but I honestly believed you were both better off without me. You wouldn't believe me if I told you how many times I tried to call you. How many times I picked up the phone or a pen, wanting to tell you how I felt, or to find out if you wanted me to come home."

They were staring at one another, neither breaking their gaze.

"It's like war made me immune to pain on so many levels, let me block things out that I shouldn't have been able to. I was putting so much energy into the younger guys serving with me sometimes, wanting to help them so bad, and at the same time ignoring what I should have been dealing with, who I should have been looking after." Now it was Luke's eyes crowded with tears, fighting to look at Ollie for fear of what he might see in hers. "My real family."

"What matters is what we do now," Ollie told him, plucking his fingers from the beer bottle and holding on tight. "We both did things we shouldn't have, but if you're prepared to start over, then so am I."

Luke had no idea what he'd done to deserve a second chance, but he wasn't going to waste it. "I know my priorities, Ollie. Now you just have to let me prove to you that it's not just about Charlie. The fact we have a son together means a lot, but it was you I fell in love with, and nothing could ever change that."

Olivia didn't want to cry, and that meant they needed to get out of here and into the open.

"Do you want to go for a walk down the beach again?"

It was as if he'd read her mind. "Sure." Even if being on the beach in the dark with him was kind of daunting.

And there were so many things she wanted to ask him, so many questions she still had, but was afraid to hear the answers to.

And she also didn't want to ruin what had been a really nice night.

She turned and waited for Luke to finish paying the bill. The beach was across the road, and standing outside, Olivia could hear the rumble of water hitting the sand. But there was one thing she knew now that she hadn't before, something that had troubled her from the day she'd found out she was pregnant, the day Luke had proposed to her.... That her husband hadn't just committed to her out of a sense of duty. Maybe he'd done it because he wanted to.

Luke appeared. "Let's go."

They walked close, side by side, but Ollie craved his touch. When he had his arm around her, it made her forget every insecurity that plagued her, made her want to exist in a world where they never discussed the tough stuff. Where him leaving wasn't an option.

Luke again seemed to read her mind, and placed his hand on the small of her back. "Do you want to sit or walk?"

She looked down and immediately wanted to sink into the cool sand.

"Sit," she said.

They walked a few feet and dropped to the ground. A little farther down the beach, a group of teens sat around a glowing campfire. The echo of their chatter drifted to them, and Olivia was pleased they weren't completely alone. It settled her jumping nerves, and gave her the confidence she needed to ask Luke a question. The final question she needed to know, to try to understand him and what his career truly meant to him.

"What was it like at war? I mean, what was it *really* like for you, Luke?"

He stiffened and she wished she'd kept her curiosity to herself. She remembered watching footage and movies of Vietnam veterans, and the one thing they'd said was that they liked to keep their memories between comrades.

"Nothing you want anyone at home to know about," said Luke, his words low and hard to hear. "It's…well, it's hard to describe."

"You don't have to tell me," she insisted. "I didn't mean to pry."

Luke turned to her, his long legs stretched out in front of him. "Ollie, you're my *wife*. If I can't tell you, then we shouldn't be sitting here together, and we sure as hell shouldn't be married."

"I just mean that…" Hell, she didn't know what she meant. The truth was that she desperately wanted to know, but still felt bad for asking him.

"Sometimes it was okay, nice even. We'd kick a ball around, talk, play cards, that sort of thing." He looked out to sea as he spoke. "Other times, the dust drove you mad, the heat made you angry, and the terror in the faces of young men who'd seen their friend killed, or witnessed something gruesome, was enough to tip you over the edge." He shook his head, as if he didn't want to confront some of those particular memories. "Special Forces was pretty exhilarating, but nothing about that was easy, either." Luke paused. "The hardest thing to describe, though, more than anything I've ever witnessed, is what it feels like to be part of that army family."

Olivia nodded. "I want to know," she told him, because maybe she'd never truly understand him if she didn't acknowledge, didn't comprehend, the way he felt about his men.

"They meant everything to me, Ollie, for so many years. The fact that I knew someone always had my back, that I always had someone around me I could count on, that I was good at what I did and could protect those guys, who would do the same for me."

Olivia had gone from wishing she'd never asked him, to wanting to talk more, to really try to understand what he'd been through, what made him the way he was.

"Iraq was full of plenty of good times, hanging out with the guys. The tour I did before I met you wasn't so good, but I can't complain. All I can say is that Delta Force took me to some places that I'd rather I hadn't seen, but it never stopped me from being grateful for the people I served with. That's the one thing I'll never be able to let go of."

Luke smiled at her, shaking his head slightly, as if he wasn't sure how else to explain it to her. "We all made a decision to put our lives in danger, to serve together, to do our duty for our country, and I guess that's what the difference is. We all knew our lives could end, and that was part of being in our army family. But being a dad and a husband? You two never signed up for that, Ollie. And I didn't want you to ever have to deal with explaining to Luke why his daddy never came home."

Olivia blinked away tears. "But that's exactly what I had to do, Luke. I had to tell him all the time that you weren't coming home, that I didn't know when we'd see you again. And that's every bit as painful as what you were scared of."

Luke dipped his head. "It wasn't until I came home that I realized that, Ollie. Which is why I can't tell you enough how sorry I am."

They sat in silence, both staring ahead. Olivia hadn't wanted to make him feel bad, to punish him all over again, but she was pleased it was out there in the open. That they were confronting their problems instead of just bottling them up inside.

"Can you tell me anything about where you were serving? What you did wherever you were?" she asked.

He shook his head, a smile touching the corner of his mouth. "Not really. But what I can tell you is that I was immersed in a culture I found terrifying, that every day I worried I'd be found out by the enemy." He shrugged. "Every guy in the army wants the bragging rights of being Delta, Special Forces, but really? It's a dangerous game of cat and mouse, and only the best survive till the end." He was staring into the distance. "But it meant a lot to the counterterrorism effort, and I'm proud of how I served our country."

"And how do you feel now?" she asked.

He turned his focus back to her. "Honestly? I miss the guys. Real bad. When you're with someone 24/7, put so much trust in what they do, it's hard not to be on that team still. But Ollie?" He looked up, a big breath making his shoulders rise, then fall. "I don't regret coming home. I'm so pleased I'm here with you again, with you and Charlie."

She didn't ask him about the future, didn't want to know how long or short a time together they might have. And in all honesty, right now, at this very moment, she didn't care. For the first time in her life, she made the first move.

Olivia reached out to touch Luke's face, her fingers splayed and resting on his cheek. And before her confidence wavered, before she could worry about what he was thinking, she leaned forward and kissed him, her lips brushing his.

Luke didn't take any convincing. He pulled her against him, his mouth hungry and possessive. He tugged her onto his lap, fitting her against him as if she was made to be in his embrace. His hands tangled in her hair, as if trying to touch as much of her as possible all at the same time, and she greedily indulged in wrapping her arms around his shoulders, kissing him for what seemed like forever.

"Get a room!"

Olivia pulled back, embarrassed. Luke rumbled with laughter. A gaggle of teens were sniggering, poking one another in the ribs as they shuffled past. Ollie tucked tight into Luke, giggling along with him even though her cheeks were burning.

He pulled her even closer, pressing one more kiss to her lips.

"What do you say?" he asked, eyes never leaving hers.

Ollie looked down, her nervousness back. Her stomach was filled with static and her mouth drier than the sand beneath her. But she needed to say yes. They did need a room. And they'd already arranged for one.

Luke helped her to her feet and they walked back to

their hotel, hand in hand. With her hair blowing in the breeze, her lips plump from all that kissing, Olivia was the happiest she'd been in as long as she could remember.

CHAPTER SIXTEEN

OLIVIA'S CONFIDENCE WAS wilting like a flower on a desperately hot day. Luke suddenly seemed too handsome, too charming, *too dangerous*. Could she cope with the heartache?

The rapid beat of her heart told another story completely. That waiting wasn't an option. Luke was her *husband*. This wasn't some one-night stand, something she should be ashamed of. This was her accepting her husband back into her life, and she wasn't going to judge herself for it.

Luke squeezed her hand and caught her eye, winking before leading her into the hotel. And in that moment she kicked the sensible fairy off her shoulder, and listened to the naughty one instead.

"No second thoughts?" he asked.

Olivia shook her head, boldly grabbing hold of the collar of his jacket and kissing his jaw. "No," she whispered.

Luke didn't need to be told twice.

He swiped the key card through the door and pushed it open for Olivia. Although they'd walked in near silence from the beach, he knew she was nervous. And so was he.

"Drink?" he asked.

She nodded. He swallowed. Their spontaneity had disappeared, turning into a nervous energy that charged between them. Luke quickly scanned the minibar, desperate for a drink of anything that would give him his courage back. He pulled out a small bottle of whiskey for himself and one of champagne for Olivia.

"Too cliché?"

"It's fine." Ollie smiled at him, her cheeks flushing pink.

Luke found a glass and poured the champagne, holding it out to her and fixing his gaze. She was his *wife,* and since when had he ever been nervous about a night with a beautiful woman?

"To us," he announced, taking a gulp of whiskey straight from the tiny bottle, trying not to grimace as it burned a hot path down his throat.

Olivia raised her glass, eyelashes hiding her round blue eyes until she was brave enough to look back at him, her chin tilted as she took a sip. "To us," she said, only now her voice was husky and low.

They both sipped again, but Luke was past needing alcohol. Or maybe the whiskey was already searing his veins, giving him the courage he'd temporarily lost when they'd first arrived back.

Only, it wasn't courage to take his wife into his arms he'd lost. It was not wanting to push her too far, in case he pushed her away. Now, he needed to know what her final decision was, and he wasn't going to play games any longer.

"Hmm, very nice choice." Olivia said as she sipped, eyes downcast again.

She was lying. He had no doubts the bubbly was average, but he didn't care.

"Luke…" she started.

He didn't have time to find out how her sentence ended.

"Ollie." His voice was deeper than he'd ever heard it, his hand closing around the whiskey bottle so hard he could have crushed it.

And it wasn't whiskey he wanted.

Luke stalked toward her, ready to claim what he *did* want, ready to kiss the gasp from her lips and crush her body against his. Olivia fell into his arms as if as desperate as he was, sliding against him as he possessed her mouth with a desperation he'd been holding back all these days. Ever since he'd arrived home.

Luke wrapped one arm around her waist, anchoring her to him despite the bottle he was still holding, his other hand searching for her face, keeping her chin tilted so she couldn't break their kiss if she tried.

Olivia was breathless, her mouth moving fast to keep up with Luke's. He pushed her roughly back onto the bed, his hungry lips, his touch even more ravenous. She arched into him, desperate to feel him against her, to carve herself into his frame.

When he pushed up, she fought not to fist her hand in his shirt and pull him down again. She didn't want him looking down at her; she wanted his body heavy over hers.

"Ollie, are you sure?"

His words surprised her. No longer shy of him, she gazed up into his honest brown eyes, at the pupils so comfortably transfixed on her own. Luke stroked her hair from her face, traced the length of her cheek and rubbed his finger over her lips, his eyes never leaving hers.

When she nodded, there was no going back. His lips found hers again, more gently this time, tender, and she sighed into his mouth as she kissed him back.

"I love you," he whispered, as he nibbled down her neck, dangerously close to the top of her bra.

I love you, too, Luke. But the words never left her mouth, because Luke's hands and mouth drifted lower, and all she could think about was that she never, ever wanted her husband to stop touching her.

Olivia tried not to surrender to sleep, but her eyelids refused to obey. Luke traced a circle around and around on her back and she snuggled closer to him, scooped into his body.

"Ollie?"

"Mmm." She could do little else other than murmur while he was touching her, her body like liquid beneath his hands.

"I thought you were asleep," he said.

Olivia opened her eyes and wriggled onto her other side so she could face him. As he stretched she ran an open palm down his chest, hovering when she reached his stomach, until in the half light she saw a thick, jagged scar that curved from the edge of his belly around his lower back.

She woke up fast, leaning forward to see how far it went. How had she not noticed this before? When he'd walked out of the bathroom before dinner?

Luke stayed still as she stared.

"How did you get this?" Her fingers wouldn't leave his skin, tracing it over and over.

"Afghanistan."

He didn't look worried about her asking, but he shut his eyes. Olivia put her hand on his chest again, her head tucked into the hollow of his arm as he flung it out over the pillow. Seeing his injury had jolted her wide-awake.

"I was shot. Had to pull the bullet out myself, then I blanked out," he told her, his tone grim. "I woke up alive, so that's what counts, and I didn't even need surgery."

She hadn't known how close she'd been to losing him

for good. That he could have died without them ever having the chance to make things right. Before she could even say goodbye to him.

"I'm glad you're home safe now," she said, tucking in tighter against him. Her only problem now was thinking about him going back again, being sent somewhere with more bullets, with more chances of him coming home in a body bag.

Luke leaned closer and dropped a kiss on her head. "Me, too."

Olivia wanted tonight to be just about them, about what they'd just shared, what had changed between them. But the idea that all this could be over when he left again, that he could die and leave her a widow? She shuddered.

"Luke, did you…I mean…"

He propped himself up on one elbow and looked down at her. She could see the question in his face, in the way his eyebrows drew closer together.

She took a deep breath and pushed it out. "Did you lose anyone close to you over there?"

The color drained out of Luke's face, but he didn't pull away.

"Yeah. I lost more than one man over there."

She didn't know what to say. Olivia just held him tighter, hoped that he would feel her strength.

"There were guys everywhere I served, guys that I lost." He paused, but she didn't look up at him. Just kept tucked into his arm as she listened. "Then when I was on my last tour, with Delta, after months and months of being undercover…"

Olivia waited. She squeezed her eyes shut as she heard his voice choke.

"I lost my partner."

She clasped him close, wanting to protect and cocoon him, yet not knowing how. What could she even say to that?

"Were you with him?"

Luke nodded his head against hers.

"He died in my arms and then I had to leave him or get killed myself."

She let him hold her tight, listened as his breathing became rapid, as if he was trying hard not to cry, before settling to a more even pace again. There was nothing she could say to make him feel better, nothing she could do. So if he wanted to hold her, then she wasn't going to move a muscle.

"Good night," he whispered, his breath soft against her ear.

"Good night," she murmured back.

Being in Luke's arms just seemed so right. And right now she didn't ever, ever want to let him go again.

CHAPTER SEVENTEEN

LUKE WAS WATCHING Olivia sleep. Her long dark eyelashes brushed her cheekbones; her mouth was parted slightly. It seemed as if he'd been like this for hours, looking at her, thinking about what he'd done.

She was the most beautiful human being he'd ever met, the kindest person he'd ever encountered. And that's why he couldn't sleep—not now and not when he'd been away.

Was he capable of giving her the life she deserved? Was he the man who could love her, hold her and cherish her forever? Was he ever going to be a good enough dad? And could he be the man he wanted to be at home and a soldier, too?

He had pain running through his chest, pulsing at his temple, gripping at his mind. It was the feeling of guilt, of loss, of terror that had plagued him every month he'd been away. Had left him awake, in a cold sweat, before he'd up and left. The guilt he'd experienced when he'd made his mind up to return to his unit, to go back to his army family. *When he'd broken his promise.* When he'd whispered goodbye to his sleeping baby, and the weight of his failure had hit him.

He'd left his family behind then because he'd had such a strong sense of duty to fight by his men, to go back to the family he'd made for himself, who'd taken him in when he'd been alone. Because he'd been so damn afraid of becoming close with his son, and then dying was the very reason he'd been determined not to be a dad at all.

He'd blamed all his issues on his upbringing, on never knowing a father figure who hadn't shown him the back of his hand. *But it wasn't that.* It was his fear of letting Olivia down. Of letting his son down. Because he hadn't believed he deserved them.

He'd been alone almost all his life, and in the army since he was barely of age. *And then he'd met Olivia.*

And now here he was again, wondering whether he could truly make a lifetime commitment to his wife and his son. Not because he wanted to be unfaithful, but because the army was his family, too. And because he'd turned down the job opportunity of a lifetime, trying to be the man he thought he should be, without even discussing it with his wife first.

Olivia started to stir and he slid back under the sheets. He held her close, touching his face to her hair, inhaling the coconut scent of her shampoo. He rubbed his lips over the so-soft skin of her neck, felt the gentle curve of her body fitted against his.

The last thing he wanted was to let her go, to lose her again. He wanted the indentation of her skin against his held in his memory forever. The taste of her lips pressed to his to be something he enjoyed every day, felt every morning when he woke up.

But he also couldn't *not* be a soldier. If that was taken away from him, then he couldn't be true to himself.

Olivia pressed into him, her body warm. Luke squeezed his eyes shut, fighting the feelings. Trying so hard to push them away.

For the first time since he was a kid, the cool slice of a

tear slid down over his cheek and hit his pillow. He wished he could push away the worry, the feeling that he didn't belong. But it was too hard.

CHAPTER EIGHTEEN

"Morning." Olivia smiled over at Luke, fighting shyness.

"Hey."

It was weird, lying naked beneath the sheets and watching her husband. Looking at him watching her, wondering what he was thinking. Wondering how he was feeling.

Last night had been amazing, *incredible,* and she couldn't believe it had happened. That she'd followed her heart instead of her mind for the first time in so long.

The half smile he gave her made her stomach knot into a tight ball.

"Is everything okay?" she asked.

Luke nodded before propping himself beside her on his elbow.

Something was wrong. Olivia's toes curled in the sheets as she tried to push the worry away.

"Ollie…"

She pulled the sheet closer to her body, a cool shiver hitting her spine.

Luke sighed, running a hand through his hair and sitting up properly. "You want to get some breakfast?"

She let the sheet fall slightly. Breakfast? He was only asking her about breakfast?

"Uh, sure." She'd been certain he was going to tell her

something deep and dark and bad. Trust her to jump to conclusions.

He got up out of bed, leaned over and gave her a kiss on the forehead. She raised her mouth, but he didn't even seem to notice. She'd been right. Something was definitely wrong.

"Luke, you sure you're okay?" She had to ask, had to know what he was thinking.

It was then that she noticed that he was already wearing boxers and his T-shirt. Had he been somewhere already? How long had she slept?

"We've said it already, but one of the reasons we couldn't be happy before was because we didn't talk enough, right? Because we couldn't just tell each other how we were feeling."

Olivia swallowed, but it was as if her tongue had swelled in her mouth, making even breathing difficult.

They'd just spent the night together. She'd fallen asleep thinking she was the luckiest girl in all the world. And now what? He was having second thoughts? "Is there something you need to tell me?"

Olivia reached for her underwear and quickly slipped it on, crossing the room to find her clothes.

"Last night was amazing, Ollie." Luke's words made her stop, hand hovering over the fresh top in her bag. "I've been awake for hours, just watching you sleep, thinking about you."

She smiled, forcing her hand from the bag so she could turn and face him. She needed to trust him, to not jump to conclusions without hearing him out first. Talking about his feelings had never been Luke's thing, so if he wanted to talk, what the hell was she doing trying to fob him off?

He walked toward her, taking her hand and walking her back to the bed. She sat down and he did the same.

"Luke, it's okay. Last night *was* great." She squeezed his hand, searching his gaze, knowing something was troubling him, and wanting so bad to know what it was. "I'm so glad we stayed."

A frown kept his mouth turned down ever so slightly at the corners, his eyes searching hers as if looking for answers, as if he had so much on his mind that he didn't know how to tell her.

"Ollie, I don't want you to take this the wrong way, but I need to talk to you about my job, instead of just bottling it all up inside and making decisions without consulting you first."

"I'm not following…." Her skin seemed instantly cool, as if she was already recoiling from what he wanted to tell her before she'd even listened to him.

"You know how important it is to me, to be a soldier, and I just don't know how to separate being a dad, a husband *and* a soldier." Luke didn't look away, kept his eyes trained on hers. "I don't want to leave you again, but I can't just give up my career, either."

Olivia couldn't help it; she glared at him, anger flaring within her. "So you're telling me that you're leaving again? That all this has been for nothing."

He shook his head, reaching out for her, cupping her cheek in his palm. "No."

She was starting to shake, just her hands, but worry—*terror*—was starting to build within her. "Luke, I get that you're a soldier, what that means to you. But you can't just leave us again, not so soon." Olivia didn't know what else to say to him, didn't know how she felt. "Am I right in guessing that any redeployment would be voluntary? Given how many tours you've been on?"

Luke nodded. "Yes."

Now she was starting to get angry. "And yet you want

to risk your life and go into the depths of hell again? *Voluntarily?*"

"I was offered a promotion within Special Forces," he told her, his voice low. "They want me to lead an elite task force and head overseas again, and I'd be lying if I told you it wasn't a position I've always dreamed of taking."

If it was possible for a human being to explode from anger, Olivia would have. "And you're telling me this now?" She was fuming.

Luke sighed, raking a hand furiously through his hair. "I didn't want to keep anything from you," he said. "I wanted to talk to you about it."

Now she was mad. Seeing-red, fists-clenched kind of mad. "Yeah, well, maybe that's a conversation we should have had last night, before you seduced me into sleeping with you." It was a low blow, but she didn't care. She'd trusted him, let herself believe in him again, and now he was telling her that he was taking his dream job?

"I stayed awake most of the night, just thinking, Ollie," he said, not meeting her eyes. "And I knew that it'd be wrong not to at least talk this through with you. But—"

She interrupted him. "No, Luke. *No*. Just stop."

His eyes were haunted, tears visible, but she didn't care. He was hurting her, not the other way around, and she didn't deserve it.

Olivia fought the tears piercing her own eyes, swallowed the sharp bite of bile in her throat, and pulled on her clothes with all the dignity she could summon. She heard Luke's voice, as if it was echoing in the background, but she didn't acknowledge him. Instead she pushed a shoe onto each foot, crossed the room to gather her things from the bathroom, and made for the door. It was over.

"Olivia, let me finish," he demanded.

She stopped, turned to stare at him. "No, Luke. This was a mistake, all of this."

"Ollie, please," he called. "Just hear me out."

But she wasn't going to listen. Not to him, not ever again. Their marriage was over. The fact that he was even thinking about leaving them told her they'd never be able to make things work between them.

She slammed the door on him. If he loved her, he'd never want to let her out of his sight.

She should never have come here with Luke, just as she should never have lost herself in the romance of being with him last night, because the only thing she'd done right since he'd returned was to tell him she wanted a divorce. If she'd stuck to her plan, none of this would have happened.

Olivia wiped her nose and brushed at her eyes, then took a few moments to steady her breathing. That was the last and only time she would cry over Luke Brown. Their marriage was finished.

Talking to his wife hadn't exactly gone as he'd planned.

Luke paced up and down the small room before looking out the window. He'd watched her go, seen her run across the street, and known he should have gone after her. Should have forced her to listen to him, tell her that he'd already turned the job down, but he knew that he needed to take some sort of active role within the army to be true to himself.

Luke pulled on his jeans and threw everything into his pack. He might have made a fool of himself just now, but he wasn't going to do it again. Not if he could help it.

If he'd just managed to get the words off his chest in the right way… Luke stopped himself. Beating himself up wasn't going to help, but he knew what would.

He picked up his phone and dialed his commanding

officer. He needed to find a way to stay loyal to his family *and* the army, and he needed to do it now. Because he couldn't be the father and husband he wanted to be if he gave up his career, if he walked away from something in his life that meant so much to him. But if he went back to being a soldier in the field? Then he may as well forget about the life he wanted to be part of here. The life that he'd fallen in love with.

His superior answered.

"Sir, it's Luke Brown here." He took a deep breath. It was now or never.

CHAPTER NINETEEN

THE PAIN DIDN'T go away, but it had faded to a dull ache. Olivia didn't want Charlie to see her cry. It had been bad enough having him ask why she had red eyes. Although the hardest question, hands down, had been "Where's Daddy?"

Kelly hadn't been so easy to fool. She'd taken one look at her and demanded to know what had happened. But talking about Luke wasn't something Olivia had any intention of doing anytime soon.

"I'm all packed up." Kelly stood in the lounge, her overnight bag hooked on her shoulder. "You sure you don't want to tell me about it?"

Olivia shook her head. Any harder and it would have fallen off.

"You sounded so happy when you phoned last night." Her friend came forward and gave her a hug. "I'm sorry, Liv. For what it's worth, I'm really, really sorry."

It wasn't that Olivia didn't want her comfort. But being enveloped in a big, caring hug made her want to sob her heart out all over again, and she wasn't going to let herself. There would be no more tears shed. Not one drop if she could help it. Because she already felt like a fool.

"Thanks so much for taking care of Charlie. I'll call you soon."

Kelly squeezed her arm one last time, eyes locked on hers, before leaving. Olivia was too exhausted to even walk her to the door. It was like she'd been on a roller coaster, over and over again, and now was physically sick and emotionally drained from it.

"Mommy!" Charlie appeared in front of her, grasping the wooden gun Luke had made for him. "Was that Daddy?"

She shook her head sadly. "No, darling, it was just Kelly leaving."

His little face fell. "Oh."

She didn't know what to say to him. Would Luke be coming past to see him again before he left? Or was it going to be like last time? Would he just disappear?

Part of her wished it had worked out, still believed it could have, but the other part? It was telling her what an idiot she'd been. He was a soldier and going away was what he did. She only wished he'd talked to her about it sooner, instead of them repeating their same old pattern.

When her mother had kept letting her father came back home, Olivia had started to think her mom was a coward. She'd vowed, even as a child, never to let anyone treat her like that. And she'd been so proud when her mom had finally kicked him out.

And yet she'd forgotten the one piece of advice her mom had given her, the one thing she should have held on tight to: that a leopard would never change its spots.

Well, she'd believed Luke had changed his, and she'd fallen for him all over again. Now she had to explain to Charlie that his dad had gone. Be honest with him that he might not come back. That he'd broken the promise he'd made to his son.

If she didn't love him so much, perhaps the pain wouldn't

feel like it was ripping her insides apart, piece by painful piece. Because this time, surely, they could have made it work.

Luke sat outside, willing himself to get out of the car. No matter what happened now, he'd made his decision. Even if Olivia said no to him, turned him away, he was going to be part of his son's life. Wasn't ever going to be serving offshore again.

The sun glinted off his windshield and Luke took it as a cue to get moving. He had no idea how Olivia would react to his turning up out of the blue, but now was as good a time as any to find out. And to tell her that he'd done something about what was keeping him from being a good dad, something that could make him a better husband.

He decided to go around the back.

Luke saw Olivia before she saw him. He took in the fall of her long, honey-brown hair, the way she so casually tucked it behind one ear as she watched Charlie. She was dressed in faded jeans and a white tank top, and she looked beautiful.

Blue eyes turned upward then, and she saw him. It wasn't the look he'd hoped for, but he guessed he deserved it. Those ocean-colored irises flashed dark—dark with hurt—and he sucked in a deep breath and walked in.

"Hi," he called out as he stood in the open back door.

"Daddy!" Charlie raced forward and threw both arms around him.

"Hey, buddy, how are you?"

Luke tried to focus on his son, but Olivia's gaze drew him. There were so many things he wanted to tell her, so much he wanted to apologize for and make up to her.

Luke didn't regret one moment of his time serving his country, but what he did regret was not calling, not being

honest, not being home with his family at every possible
interval. But he'd done the right thing now, no matter what
Ollie decided about their future, and he could finally say,
with his hand on his heart, that he could be the dad his
son deserved.

"Ollie—" He was interrupted.

"Daddy, are you home now? Are you staying here?
Mommy said you might be going away again!"

Luke dropped to his knees and cupped his hand under
his son's chin before touching foreheads with him.

"I need to talk with your mom, okay?" he said in a low
voice. "But I'm not leaving you, kiddo. I promise. Not now
and not ever."

"Really?" Charlie asked, eyes unblinking as he stared
up at him.

"I made you a promise, son. I said that if I ever left
again, you'd know when and where I was going. I'm not
gonna break that promise. Okay?"

Charlie seemed satisfied. "'Kay."

Luke sensed rather than heard Olivia tsk, but he kept
his eyes on his boy. When Charlie smiled, he dropped a
kiss on his head and stood to full height. Olivia thought
he was making false promises, but he wasn't. Not this
time, not *ever.*

Because this time, he was playing for keeps. And he
wasn't going to take no for an answer.

"You go play in your room for a moment, bud. What
I've got to say to Mommy won't take long."

Olivia stood like a soldier, and Luke wondered if she
knew her habit. Feet spread hip-width apart, arms crossed,
steely gaze, chin tilted. He'd never known such a strong
woman in all his life.

"So you're here to say goodbye." It was a statement
more than a question.

"No." Had she thought he was lying to Charlie just then? Did she honestly believe that he would have spent the night with her if he'd planned on shipping out without consulting her first?

Olivia didn't look convinced, eyes still narrowed in his direction.

"Ollie, I'm here to ask your forgiveness," he said, taking a few steps closer to her. "I should never have just come out with what was on my mind before, without explaining where it was coming from, why I was thinking about it."

"Why? So you can leave with a clear conscience?" The snap of her tone made him stop moving closer.

"No." He looked at his feet, then back up at her. "Because I love you and I want to be part of your life. Because I want to stay."

"Why should I believe you this time, Luke? Why?"

He knew she was hurt. He'd been the one to hurt her, and if he could take that moment in time back, then he damn well would. This was hard for him, too, but he wasn't backing down.

Luke took a deep breath. "Because no matter what happens, Ollie, I'm staying. I'm not going to serve overseas again, not now and not ever. That's what I was trying to talk to you about."

Now it was Olivia who wanted to run. After all this time of being the strong one, of being the woman who could cope on her own and who didn't need help, she was crumbling. Tears were stinging her eyes and a lump was steadily moving its way up her throat.

She wanted to yell at Luke, to beat her fists against his chest till it hurt him, to tell him to walk out that door and never come back. But she couldn't.

Because she loved him. He was her husband, the father

of her child and her first love. And because once again she'd let him down by not listening to him.

"I can't keep going on like this, Luke," she said. "If you say you're staying, then I need to know that you mean it."

He towered over her, looking more determined than she'd ever seen him. "Ollie, I'm staying and I love you. It's that simple."

"Saying it and meaning it are two different things." Her words were strong, her tears had faded and her voice had regained its full power. "I trusted you last night, Luke, but…" She swallowed, nodding her head to make herself continue. "You can't pretend to be someone you're not, just for our sake. I want you to be happy as much as I want Charlie to be happy, and I know that you'll never be content if you have to leave the army behind."

The look on his face made her heart pound, loudly, as if it was in her ears and not her chest.

"I meant what I said to you yesterday, last night," he told her. "I meant every word."

"What did you mean when you said you were staying?" Olivia asked, needing to know, wanting to know if it was actually possible.

"That I'm here, Ollie. For good this time. I promise I'm not going anywhere unless you and Charlie are with me." Luke smiled as he looked at her. "I came back here to re-connect with my son, but I realized when I got back that that wasn't enough. I want the whole package, and that means you *and* Charlie."

"I don't believe you." She shifted her weight from one foot to the other. The nature of the army didn't let that be an option, and Luke was a soldier. "You can't just change who you are, Luke."

"The only reason I didn't get here sooner is because I've been negotiating a new position," Luke told her, a smile taking over his mouth. "I've been completely released from active duty in exchange for taking over a training role, here on home soil. We'll need to move close to base, so it does mean a change, but I'm not leaving you, Ollie. I'm not leaving you or Charlie, no matter what. I want you both by my side, now and always."

Olivia's heart hiccuped, as if it actually stopped beating, then reignited. *Staying?* Did he mean it this time? Her first instinct was to tell him no, to avoid being hurt, in case what he said wasn't true. But the truth was that the moment she'd heard his words, she'd started to hope. Truly hope. Because all along Luke had been torn between his home family and his army family, and him being part of both meant she wouldn't have to lose him again. That he wouldn't have to make a choice that ruined either his family or his career.

"What base?" She had to ask, had to know the realities.

"Fort Bragg." He took her hand, staring straight into her eyes. "I don't know yet if we'd be living on base or off, but I want us to do this together, if you'll come with me." He sighed, never breaking their gaze. "I don't want to do this without you, Ollie. Without either of you."

Olivia felt what she knew was a dangerous emotion: real hope. It had resurfaced, and no matter how hard she tried to push it down, it was fluttering around her. Beating in her ears so she couldn't avoid it.

CHAPTER TWENTY

OLLIE STILL LOOKED angry, but Luke had a fire in his belly that he knew couldn't be extinguished. Not now that he'd finally opened up and changed the path of his life to keep his family *and* his career. It was like the rush of first love, but even stronger.

"Olivia," he said, forcing his voice to stay steady. He prised her other hand from her hip, needing to hold both her hands in his for what he was about to say, needing to know that she was going to be by his side, now and always. "Olivia, will you marry me?"

She looked as if he'd asked her to go giraffe riding.

"Marry you?"

Luke smiled, unable to help himself, before dropping to one knee.

"I know we're already married, but I want a fresh beginning, to be the husband I should have been." His voice caught on the emotion in his throat. "I love you, baby. I love you so much and I can't believe what a fool I've been for so long. This is about me making a decision for us, so we don't have to be apart. So that we can move on and be a real family."

Her mouth hung open, as if her jaw muscles had disintegrated. As if she didn't know what to say or how to say it.

"What do you say, Ollie? Will you give me a second chance to be the man I know I can be?"

As she finally met his eyes, looked at him with the expression he'd hoped for, a little voice called out, so loud it made him turn.

"Say yes, Mommy! Say you'll marry Daddy again!"

A cheeky face was watching them from the doorway. Luke gave his son a wink and stood in front of his wife, knowing that it was now or never, that he was finally doing the right thing.

"What do you say, Ollie?" he asked. "Will you do me the honor of being my wife?"

"Yes," she whispered, so only he could hear. "Yes, Luke, I will."

Tears flowed freely down her cheeks and he pulled her close, enveloped her in his arms. He only wished he never had to let her go.

"Do you mean it, Luke?" she asked as she leaned back in his arms. "Do you promise you'll be that man? Do you promise you'll never, *ever* leave us like that again? That we'll be a family this time?"

"I promise, honey," he said into her ear. "I've never meant something so much in all my life. *I love you.*"

"It was never about you fighting for what you believed in, Luke. I would never ask you to stop being a soldier. You know that, don't you?"

"I know, baby. I know."

Charlie hurtled full steam into them, throwing his arms around their legs before Luke even had a chance to kiss her. He bent to grab him, pulling him up onto his hip.

"You said yes?" Charlie asked.

Ollie nodded and Luke squeezed him tightly.

"My second-chance soldier," she said, her voice still choked with tears as she held them both.

"Believe me when I say we won't need any more chances," Luke said, kissing first his wife, then his son.

His family.

EPILOGUE

THE BAR WAS QUIET, filled with a few off-duty soldiers and a handful of civilians. Luke smiled as he ordered a round and then stepped back over to his table. They were so full of enthusiasm, so young, that he almost felt guilty. The feeling passed, but his affection for them didn't.

The young men he trained had become his family, his de facto sons for the period of time he spent with them. His superiors would say he became far too attached to them, too fond of them for anyone's good, but Luke disagreed. He'd heard the same thing said about police dog handlers, and he didn't believe in staying detached, not for a moment.

These guys sitting before him, crowded into a booth, were ready to ship out at any moment, to defend their country at all costs. He didn't know where they'd end up, but he wanted them to leave knowing what was important, and knowing how proud they should be of themselves.

Luke placed the beers on the table.

"You staying around tonight, sir?"

Luke laughed. He hated them calling him sir, but that was one army rule he wasn't brave enough to flout.

"No, fellas, I've got someone waiting for me."

"Ooh," they all chorused, erupting into laughter.

Luke shook his head and let them laugh. He didn't care

if they wanted to make fun of him. He probably would have, too, at the same age.

"You know what, boys?"

They looked back at him, most of them grinning.

"Don't forget about what's important when you get posted. Call your parents, your girlfriends, your wives. Write letters. Don't forget that those people are what pull you through the tough times."

That seemed to get their attention. None of the boys here tonight had come from the kind of background he'd had, so they probably didn't have the issues he'd been burdened with as a rookie soldier. But he bet they had days where they didn't realize how much their families meant to them. And he wanted to change that.

"I learned the hard way, and I wish I'd had someone around to tell me that before I left. To tell me how precious those people are, and that no matter how scared you are about what you're going through, you can't block them out."

He saw a few of them look up, their attention distracted. One of them whistled. Luke grinned, turning in his seat. He would bet the next round of drinks he knew who they were looking at.

Olivia stood in the doorway, half concealed by the darkness. Her long, dark hair hung around her shoulders; and her slender figure was encased in tight jeans and a simple cotton top. When she saw Luke she smiled and made her way over. He rose, winking at the boys.

He reached for his wife when she neared them, pulled her close and planted a kiss on her lips. Ollie half heartedly tried to slap at him, before laughing and resting her forehead against his.

"Don't forget what I said," he called over his shoulder. "Never forget what you're fighting for."

They walked out to the sound of whoops behind them. Luke put his hand on Ollie's bottom, but she pushed it off just as fast and swatted at him again.

"I love you, baby," he said into her ear.

"I know," she replied, smiling over at him. "I love you, too."

Luke pulled open the door and followed her out. He was proud of being a soldier, and he was proud of being a dad, but what he loved most of all was being a husband.

Pity it had taken him so darn long to figure it out.

* * * * *

Mills & Boon® Hardback
March 2013

ROMANCE

Playing the Dutiful Wife	Carol Marinelli
The Fallen Greek Bride	Jane Porter
A Scandal, a Secret, a Baby	Sharon Kendrick
The Notorious Gabriel Diaz	Cathy Williams
A Reputation For Revenge	Jennie Lucas
Captive in the Spotlight	Annie West
Taming the Last Acosta	Susan Stephens
Island of Secrets	Robyn Donald
The Taming of a Wild Child	Kimberly Lang
First Time For Everything	Aimee Carson
Guardian to the Heiress	Margaret Way
Little Cowgirl on His Doorstep	Donna Alward
Mission: Soldier to Daddy	Soraya Lane
Winning Back His Wife	Melissa McClone
The Guy To Be Seen With	Fiona Harper
Why Resist a Rebel?	Leah Ashton
Sydney Harbour Hospital: Evie's Bombshell	Amy Andrews
The Prince Who Charmed Her	Fiona McArthur

MEDICAL

NYC Angels: Redeeming The Playboy	Carol Marinelli
NYC Angels: Heiress's Baby Scandal	Janice Lynn
St Piran's: The Wedding!	Alison Roberts
His Hidden American Beauty	Connie Cox

ROMANCE

A Night of No Return	Sarah Morgan
A Tempestuous Temptation	Cathy Williams
Back in the Headlines	Sharon Kendrick
A Taste of the Untamed	Susan Stephens
The Count's Christmas Baby	Rebecca Winters
His Larkville Cinderella	Melissa McClone
The Nanny Who Saved Christmas	Michelle Douglas
Snowed in at the Ranch	Cara Colter
Exquisite Revenge	Abby Green
Beneath the Veil of Paradise	Kate Hewitt
Surrendering All But Her Heart	Melanie Milburne

HISTORICAL

How to Sin Successfully	Bronwyn Scott
Hattie Wilkinson Meets Her Match	Michelle Styles
The Captain's Kidnapped Beauty	Mary Nichols
The Admiral's Penniless Bride	Carla Kelly
Return of the Border Warrior	Blythe Gifford

MEDICAL

Her Motherhood Wish	Anne Fraser
A Bond Between Strangers	Scarlet Wilson
Once a Playboy...	Kate Hardy
Challenging the Nurse's Rules	Janice Lynn
The Sheikh and the Surrogate Mum	Meredith Webber
Tamed by her Brooding Boss	Joanna Neil

Mills & Boon® Hardback

April 2013

ROMANCE

Master of her Virtue	Miranda Lee
The Cost of her Innocence	Jacqueline Baird
A Taste of the Forbidden	Carole Mortimer
Count Valieri's Prisoner	Sara Craven
The Merciless Travis Wilde	Sandra Marton
A Game with One Winner	Lynn Raye Harris
Heir to a Desert Legacy	Maisey Yates
The Sinful Art of Revenge	Maya Blake
Marriage in Name Only?	Anne Oliver
Waking Up Married	Mira Lyn Kelly
Sparks Fly with the Billionaire	Marion Lennox
A Daddy for Her Sons	Raye Morgan
Along Came Twins…	Rebecca Winters
An Accidental Family	Ami Weaver
A Date with a Bollywood Star	Riya Lakhani
The Proposal Plan	Charlotte Phillips
Their Most Forbidden Fling	Melanie Milburne
The Last Doctor She Should Ever Date	Louisa George

MEDICAL

NYC Angels: Unmasking Dr Serious	Laura Iding
NYC Angels: The Wallflower's Secret	Susan Carlisle
Cinderella of Harley Street	Anne Fraser
You, Me and a Family	Sue MacKay

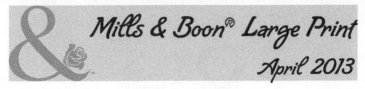

ROMANCE

A Ring to Secure His Heir	Lynne Graham
What His Money Can't Hide	Maggie Cox
Woman in a Sheikh's World	Sarah Morgan
At Dante's Service	Chantelle Shaw
The English Lord's Secret Son	Margaret Way
The Secret That Changed Everything	Lucy Gordon
The Cattleman's Special Delivery	Barbara Hannay
Her Man in Manhattan	Trish Wylie
At His Majesty's Request	Maisey Yates
Breaking the Greek's Rules	Anne McAllister
The Ruthless Caleb Wilde	Sandra Marton

HISTORICAL

Some Like It Wicked	Carole Mortimer
Born to Scandal	Diane Gaston
Beneath the Major's Scars	Sarah Mallory
Warriors in Winter	Michelle Willingham
A Stranger's Touch	Anne Herries

MEDICAL

A Socialite's Christmas Wish	Lucy Clark
Redeeming Dr Riccardi	Leah Martyn
The Family Who Made Him Whole	Jennifer Taylor
The Doctor Meets Her Match	Annie Claydon
The Doctor's Lost-and-Found Heart	Dianne Drake
The Man Who Wouldn't Marry	Tina Beckett

0313 GEN STD LP